"Where did you go when you were in high school and wanted to make out?"

Signey frowned at his words. "They've built a shopping mall there." The rough texture of Jess's thumb tracing her lip broke any self-control Signey had. She should leave, but she couldn't.

His lips brushed her ear. "I want you." Then he kissed her, not teasing and light as before, but long and hard.

Her response matched his, scaring her. "Jess, no." He faced death every time he walked into a rodeo arena.

Jess knew the real reason for her resistance. "People get killed crossing the street, Signey."

Miserably, Signey shook her head. She couldn't live with her fear for Jess.

Jess cupped her face in his strong hand and raised her eyes to his and smiled wickedly. "But you don't know how good I am...."

It was only natural that **Carly Bishop** would eventually write about a cowboy and a spunky heroine. After all, she grew up in Cheyenne, Wyoming, with an uncle who was a bullrider, and spent her formative years watching Clint Eastwood on *Rawhide*. And what a great cowboy Jess Hawkins is! A man who loves women and fights for what's right. Carly has found her own hero, and they live in Denver with a lovely daughter.

Books by Carly Bishop

HARLEQUIN INTRIGUE
170–FUGITIVE HEART

HARLEQUIN DREAMSCAPE
PRINCE OF DREAMS

Going For It!

CARLY BISHOP

Harlequin Books

TORONTO • NEW YORK • LONDON
AMSTERDAM • PARIS • SYDNEY • HAMBURG
STOCKHOLM • ATHENS • TOKYO • MILAN

To my dad, who taught me to go for it,
and to my mom, who gave me the freedom

Published December 1991

ISBN 0-373-25476-8

GOING FOR IT!

1

"YOUR TICKET, PLEASE?"

Anticipation surged through Signey Jensen. She'd been tempted to jump the unexpectedly long line by flashing her press credentials, and collecting her boarding pass for Cheyenne, Wyoming. Something had held her back.

She passed her ticket to the clerk. Today, for the first time in ten years, she was going home.

"Jensen, Jensen," he muttered, stabbing at the computer keys. The reservations agent peered at her above the half glasses that kept sliding down his nose. "Say, aren't you the hostess of the morning news show ... what's it called, uh, 'Good Morning' ...?"

"Hostess?" Signey laughed. The word was too reminiscent of cupcakes for her liking, but she had grown used to it. "No, not exactly. I'm with Cable Sports. Do you know the network?"

"Oh, yeah! You wouldn't be heading on up to cover the rodeo, now would you?"

"Exactly." Cheyenne held the largest outdoor rodeo anywhere. She'd cut her teeth around rodeos, where life was uncomplicated, men were cowboys, and cowboys were heroes. "I'm doing interest pieces. In-depth interviews. Behind the scenes. Newsmagazine sorts of topics."

"Well, that's great. Anyhow, there are a few seats available, but your friend canceled the reservation."

"Canceled? Someone canceled my reservation?"

"He assured me that you'd made other plans!"

Marshaling her dwindling good humor, Signey ran her fingers over the cloisonné surface of the tiny hand mirror in her jacket pocket. "He who?"

"The man over there." The clerk gestured, his glasses slipping another notch. "The one with the flashy turquoise watch and the fly-boy sunglasses."

Signey turned. Crowds of July travelers, harried parents and kids on vacation temporarily blocked her line of vision. As they moved on she caught sight of him.

Leaning against a post he wore reflective aviator glasses and a turquoise-imbedded silver watch. A Stetson shadowed his face. His stance was all male, his athletic bearing controlled, confident.

Hawkins. Flares of awareness burst inside her. Jess Hawkins. Every woman's cowboy hero—in the flesh. Hawkins had ridden bulls in enough pro rodeo championships to be a legend. He drew the attention of every passing female older than twelve. But that didn't tell even half the story. He radiated quiet strength. He exuded power.

"Ms. Jensen, shall I issue you another boarding pass?" the agent asked.

Signey waffled. There were others waiting impatiently in line behind her. She had to decide. Hawkins unfolded his arms for long enough to tip his hat to her, and amusement seized her. Hawkins might have been a great bull rider but he was in serious need of a good comeuppance.

Abandoning her place, she considered veering off in another direction to get a reaction from him, but she didn't. Beating him at his own game seemed like a whole lot more fun. Let him think she hadn't the least idea who he was.

"Have we met?" she demanded sweetly.

Hawkins laughed. "That memorable, huh?"

"I have an excellent memory," she said. Of his voice, for instance, and his laughter. His body. She recalled more than she was strictly comfortable with.

She took her time perusing his features. Hair the color of wheat in the late-afternoon sun brushed his collar. His jaw was square with a deep cleft in his chin. A thin, nearly invisible scar marked his right cheek. It irritated her that she couldn't tell if her brazen appraisal had any effect.

"Maybe not," he taunted softly.

She'd lost her train of thought altogether. "Maybe not what?"

"Your memory," he prodded, smiling at her.

Her chin rose. "Try me."

"I'd like that."

"What makes you think so?" The suggestion of intimacy in his gravelly baritone played on her nerves, and her fingers traced patterns in her cloisonné-backed mirror.

"The challenge."

"What challenge?"

"Hands Off. Off Limits. No Trespassing. You have warning labels sticking out all over the place." Idly he removed his aviator glasses and let them fall to his chest on a cord a more insecure cowboy would have considered sissy.

"C'mon, Signey. Madison Square Garden. You won my national finals belt buckle fair and square, and then refused to take it."

She remembered. She'd been covering a rodeo. Broken leg and all, he'd been the color commentator. On the other hand, she had forgotten what it felt like to be challenged on more than a verbal level.

But the gig was up. "Hawkins, I presume?"

"Why do I get the feeling you knew that all along?"

"Don't pout, Hawkins. It doesn't become you."

"I never pout."

"Uh-huh." His eyes trailed all over her face. If she'd won this battle of wills, why was he looking at her like that?

"So tell me. Do warning labels mean anything to you?" She sensed that Hawkins ignored a warning as simple as Beware of Dog.

"Not usually."

"Why did you cancel my reservation?"

"I'm headed to Montana. Thought I'd offer you a lift."

"Not Frontier Days?"

"Cheyenne's on the way."

The words yes and no seemed not to be in his vocabulary. "And you didn't think to ask before rearranging my plans?" Of course, she knew better. Hawkins was the sort to act now and ask questions later. "Look, I hardly know you—"

He held out his hand and Signey found her own enveloped. Her fingers were cold. His were warm as sunlight on the prairie. "Jess Hawkins," he recited. "Age—"

"Thirty-six?" she interrupted. "Born and raised in Reno, Nevada. Three-time bull-riding champion of the world, five times national rodeo finals all-around cowboy. Retired now, if you're not going to rodeo in Cheyenne. Oh, and ranching . . . near Reno? Does that about cover the territory?"

Jess let out a low, surprised whistle. "Most of it. I guess I should be flattered."

"Don't be," Signey answered. "Remember, I have an excellent memory." She found her good humor returning. "Look, all I really want is to get on a plane."

"That's fine."

Her pulse began a curious two-step beat. "That's fine?"

"Sure. My F-33 Bonanza. Which is why I didn't ask first. One flier to another, I didn't think you'd mind."

A Bonanza was the flying equivalent to a Mercedes-Benz, and she'd rather fly in a single-engine plane than cover the next Olympics. A thrill curled through her, as did suspicion. "How did you know?"

"That you're a flier?" He grinned. "Unnamed sources."

"But why do you want to fly me home?"

He smiled, clearly pleased with himself and her reaction. "I wanted to talk. Privately."

"Talk."

"Yeah, talk. What do you say? Will you fly with me?"

Given half a chance, and access to a Bonanza—any day. It was impossible to work up an honest temper over his gambit. Creative license, that was what it was—like the first time she'd connived her way into the locker room of a college football team.

He only wanted to talk, but he'd gone to extraordinary lengths to do so.

Strategy.

Timing.

She was drawn to Hawkins by those talents. Recklessness argued for flying with him, caution, against. "My luggage . . ."

"It's taken care of. All you have to do is say yes."

"On one condition—that I get to do the flying."

His smile acknowledged her willpower. "You drive a hard bargain, Signey."

"I fly even better."

"Good enough." He tucked her hand into the crook of his arm, and giving up caution as a lost cause, she accompanied Hawkins through the airport to his plane.

BELTED INTO the pilot's seat of the Bonanza thirty minutes later, Signey was where he wanted her—alone with him, his captive audience. Jess wished he knew how the hell to start.

"November-Tango-One-Niner-Four-Niner, please hold for instructions."

Signey radioed her assent. He watched, warding off the impulse to touch her. She had fair skin without the mass of freckles so common to redheads—even strawberry blondes like her. She had delicate features and a lone, inviting freckle on the lobe of her right ear.

He needed to remember the lady had grit, not the fact that she also possessed an enchanting freckle that begged to be kissed. That was why he'd taken the trouble to find her, offering a plane ride. There weren't many places more private than the cabin of a single-engined plane, and he really did need to talk.

The tower controller interrupted his thoughts. "Niner-Four-Niner, you are cleared for takeoff. Proceed to . . ."

Jess watched Signey as she prepared for takeoff, her motions as practiced and familiar as if she'd been shoving off on a bike. He didn't usually let anyone fly his bird but he was desperate. And Signey was good.

The rumbling vibrations of the wheels against the tarmac reached to the pit of his stomach. Signey relaxed in the brown, tweed-covered seat as she held Jess's plane, at his advice, to around 95 knots to gain the assigned altitude. When she'd leveled off, Signey checked the instrument panel one last time, then glanced out her window.

"The prairie always surprises me—so stark, so dry." Her quiet pleasure was obvious to Jess. "In the South everything is so green."

He nodded. "You live in Atlanta?" He knew she did.

"Yeah. Cable Sports doesn't require that I live there, but it's always seemed easier. I grew up in Cheyenne."

He knew that, too. "Do you still have family there?"

"My parents have a ranch there. They spend the summer in Jackson Hole, though. I'll have the house to myself."

"Won't they come down to Cheyenne, if you'll be home for a couple of weeks?"

"No. They call on my birthday, I call on Thanksgiving and Christmas. Daddy thinks I do everything the hard way, Mom thinks I won't understand her until I have babies of my own. Since babies are not in my foreseeable future, we have very little to talk about." Signey lightened her grip on the yoke. "Do you really own this plane?"

Jess accepted the change of subject. "I've owned it since Beech Aircraft rolled 'er off the assembly line. Do you? Do things the hard way?"

Disbelieving his nerve, Signey nodded. "Today, for instance. It would have been a lot easier to take my original connecting flight."

"Ah, but you don't get to pilot nearly enough."

"Not nearly," she agreed. "Renting by the hour leaves a lot to be desired. But I love it. I've had my license since I was sixteen, and before that it was a swing."

"A swing?"

"Yeah . . . when I was a kid," Signey continued. "An old wooden swing hanging in a tree. I was in the thing so much, the ropes wore through one of the branches. Daddy wanted to build me a tree house instead. I just picked another branch for the swing. A higher one."

He wondered if she'd ever played house. "How high?"

Her cheeky smile broadened. "I had to use a stepladder to get to it."

"Little daredevil, weren't you?"

Signey cast him a quick glance. Someone might have told him she'd fly, given a pair of water wings. No one could have revealed how very undaredevillike she'd become. "You're the card-carrying daredevil, Hawkins. I gave it up with braces and a ponytail."

He didn't believe it. He'd heard stories about her taking on causes that scared away lesser souls. And he wanted to know why she claimed to have given it up. "So you're doing what . . . faking it?"

Signey laughed softly and nodded, remembering. "Exactly. When I learned to fly—when I went on my first solo flight—I couldn't stop wondering what in the world I was doing. Like, who do you think you are, Signey Jensen, flying up here all by yourself? My Grandma Jensen always used to say to me, 'Signey Marie, *pretend* like you're brave enough and then you will be!' So . . . yeah. I guess you could say I was, that I *am* faking it."

Jess had angled his body, back to the door, so that he could watch her more closely. A strand of her hair had fallen forward, and he reached out to tuck it behind her ear. "I think I like Grandma Jensen already."

"Past tense," she told him. "She died two years ago. She was eighty-seven years old." And still there were times Signey picked up her phone, wanting only to talk to Grandma Jensen.

Jess understood the loss. "I know how it is. My dad died last February. For me," he went on, "it's easier knowing he'd be happy that I've gone back to ranching. Grandma Jensen must have died happy, knowing you're so accomplished at faking it."

He didn't know the half of how accomplished she was. "Hawkins?"

"Call me Jess, Signey."

He looked straight at her, and his smile unnerved her. In defense she raised her chin. "How did you know where to find me?"

"I called Corporate in Atlanta yesterday and asked for you. The switchboard transferred my call to Martha Chin's office."

"*Martha's* office? You're on a first-name basis with the network dragon lady?"

"Why not?"

"It just doesn't happen."

If the savvy, self-proclaimed inscrutable Martha Chin had fallen so quickly to Hawkins's handling, Signey had even more reason to feel threatened by his smiles.

"What's so important that Martha gave you my itinerary?"

"Nothing I wanted to go into with her. I just told her we were old family friends."

"And the truth?"

"The truth is, I wanted to get your take on Walter Finley."

Surprised, Signey ran her thumbs along the control yoke. "My opinion is pretty much a matter of record. Walter Finley owns Cable Sports, a football franchise in New Jersey, and the race cars Dave Lindstrom drives. He gives lip service to a drug-free America, raises championship setters, and regularly mouths off about his competitors."

"None of which tells me what *you* think of him. Come on, Signey. Don't you trust me?"

"I don't even know you, Hawkins."

"Jess," he corrected again. "I'm the guy in the white hat."

"Ha! For your information, Jesse James pillaged the West in a white hat."

Signey tried to resist the pleasing sound of Jess's laughter.

"Is that true?"

"I don't know," she said, "but it sounds good."

"Yeah. There's a difference, though. I pillage more selectively than my namesake."

"Pillage elsewhere, Hawkins," she warned.

He gave her a don't-bet-the-farm-on-it grin that faded almost as fast as it had appeared. "I wouldn't ask about Finley if it weren't important."

"I think he's nearly pathological when it comes to winning. I think he's shaky, unstable, maybe."

Jess nodded. Dave Lindstrom, the race-car driver she'd listed in Finley's résumé, was Jess's brother-in-law and an old friend of Signey's.

"So if you feel that way about Finley, why do you stay with Cable Sports?"

Signey shrugged. "There aren't a lot of jobs like mine out there, and I love it . . . Jess. On a day-to-day basis, I rarely have to deal with Finley. He doesn't appreciate my style of reporting, but Cable Sports would fold without Martha Chin. As executive editor, she calls the shots."

"Including who works for her and who doesn't?"

"Yes." Signey noticed that he wore the turquoise-embedded watchband on his right wrist. A southpaw. Nothing about Hawkins was at all ordinary.

"In Las Vegas last year the bookies were giving seven-to-one odds your 'Heroes Are Human, Too' piece would be the end of your career at Cable Sports."

"Jimmy Carver is a sucker for the underdog—especially if it's a woman." Signey corrected her controls for a gust of wind. Carver was the kingpin of Las Vegas odds makers. "My commentary was just making the point that some owners push their athletes too far. I never mentioned Finley's name."

"But he took it personally."

"I wish he'd taken it to heart, Jess. There are things more important than the winning and the almighty dollar."

"What if he'd pulled your contract?"

Her shoulder rose again. "Some things are worth standing up for. I suppose Carver thought I was foolish?" Signey continued. She knew he had zero tolerance for fools.

"Not foolish." Jess glanced quickly over all his indicators, then fixed his eyes upon her. "Fearless."

Fearless. Signey almost laughed. Either the world needed a reality check, or she'd made deception into an art form. "What's this all about, Jess? Who cares?"

Jess searched her delicate features for a moment, looking for the fleeting panic he'd seen only seconds before. Another strong gust of wind forced her to make another adjustment to the plane's course, and he realized with a small shock how comfortable he'd been with her at the controls.

"Dave Lindstrom crashed in one of Finley's experimental cars, Signey."

He knew a fair man would have come out with that a lot sooner, but he didn't always play fair. He'd wanted to find out how strongly she believed in the words she had delivered so well to a national audience.

"No!" Her stomach knotted. She had never quite outgrown the eleven-year-old who'd seen her brother crash on his skis into a tree at seventy-some miles an hour. "Dave's—"

"Fine. Got away without a scratch. None that you can see, anyway."

Signey shivered. "You think Finley is somehow at fault?"

Though he'd set her up to add two and two, Jess was uncomfortable with the sum of it himself. "I don't know, but when a man is shaken up like Dave is, sometimes he looks for someone to blame, when maybe it's his own nerve he's lost."

"Surely you can't believe that!" She'd covered Dave Lindstrom's rookie Indy 500 win on her first time out for Cable Sports. She knew how good he was, knew Dave wasn't the kind who easily lost his nerve.

"No. But it's hard to imagine how Finley could be involved. Dave's the one who crashed the car."

"Unless the car was sabotaged."

She supposed it said a lot about Finley that such a suggestion didn't seem ridiculous. He was capable of resorting to desperate measures. She'd seen Finley lie when the truth would have been safer.

Jess nodded thoughtfully. "Sabotage is a definite possibility. But why? Why deliberately destroy a race car and risk Dave's life?"

"Is there a financial angle—an insurance scam or a tax write-off?" Signey hesitated. "Wait a minute.... How are you involved?"

"I haven't talked to him about any of this. He's told Kelly, in the privacy of their bedroom. Kelly is my little sister. She's pregnant and scared for him... We're close enough to Cheyenne that you'd better initiate contact with the ground control."

"Kelly is your sister?" Automatically, Signey radioed her coordinates, ETA and requested approach instructions. Then, waiting for ground control to respond, she wondered why Kelly had never said Jess Hawkins was her brother. "So Dave didn't tell you any of this, but Kelly did? She must be very upset. She's not doing very well with this pregnancy."

"She's not having an easy time of it, that's true. And she doesn't get shook up easily. The problem is that she's never seen Dave get shaken, either."

"Did she ask you to help?"

"Actually, she asked me to keep it to myself."

Before he could explain why he hadn't, the tower responded and Signey turned her full attention to adjusting to the traffic pattern, preparing for the left-base approach.

Jess pointed out the nonstandard placement of the landing-gear switch and indicator lights, then watched in approval as she back-throttled to make an over-the-fence approach. Moments later they turned onto the taxi strip.

The engine hadn't fully powered down before Jess opened the door, vaulted onto the tarmac, then turned to offer her a hand. He went back for her luggage and blocked the wheels. Signey wondered if he regretted confiding in her.

Ten minutes later, with a baggage handler dispatched and the keys to a rented Ford LTD in her hands, she stood leaning against the open car door. She finally had Hawkins's full attention again.

"Is there anything I can do?"

Jess lifted his Stetson, dragged a hand through his hair, then resettled his hat. It had begun to cloud over, and the air smelled of the coming rain. He needed to get off the ground soon. Then again, being with Signey Jensen was about as pleasant a way to spend an afternoon as he'd done in a very long time. He was thinking up excuses to stay when she prodded him again.

"Hawkins? What can I do?"

Jess reluctantly shook off his thoughts of spending more time near her just for the hell of it. "Dave's taken Kelly and the kids to stay with his folks in San Diego for a couple of days. At this point, as long as he isn't driving, nothing much can happen. I guess I just wanted someone else to know. Someone who's in Dave's corner, who knows him and cares, in case this turns out to be more than an accident." He looked Signey squarely in her doe-brown eyes. "I thought you might be that person. Was I wrong?"

He thought she was fearless. A daredevil. He was wrong about that, but not about her loyalty to Dave. "No. You weren't wrong."

The wind gusted, carrying a stronger scent of rain, and blew Signey's strawberry-blond hair across her lips. Jess reached out and guided the errant strands away. He felt her shiver and hoped it was from his touch and not the sharp breeze.

"And you don't think Dave's imagining things?"

The man should have been whispering sweet nothings from the way she was reacting. Signey nodded and took a tiny step back from him. "I wouldn't put any kind of scam past Finley. But he's smart, and any evidence will be so buried an outside audit won't prove much. Can you talk to Kelly again? Encourage her to get Dave to talk to you—or me? We won't know how to begin unless he's willing to tell us what he suspects."

"Sure, I can do that."

"Maybe he should look at the practice tapes, too."

"Videos? They videotape practice runs?"

"Finley's penthouse office at Corporate in Atlanta has a library full of them. Surely Dave sees them?"

"I have heard him talk about them. I'll see if he's done that."

For a second, Signey was acutely aware of the silence between them, of the wind whining and the birds screeching from their swinging perches. "Hawkins?"

"Yeah?"

"You could have saved yourself a lot of time and trouble with a phone call."

"I tried that, remember? I just got Martha Chin."

The baggage handler arrived to load Signey's gear into the trunk. Jess crowded her body with his, moving her farther into the V made by the open door. His fingers took hold of her chin, making it impossible not to look into his eyes. "I'm glad you flew with me."

His gravelly voice hinted at more, and Signey felt a bolt of awareness. Sexual and unsettling, the feeling lingered. Flying had nothing to do with it. She suspected that if he'd offered a bicycle built for two, she'd have gone along.

His thumbs stroked her earlobe, while his fingers curled around the back of her neck. Wanton awareness flashed through her, and she could think of nothing to fill the silence between them.

Her stupid, highly paid, gilded tongue moistened her lips. Hawkins lowered his head and his clever, unpaid, naked tongue finished the job with impudent little swipes.

She forgot to breathe. One taste of him and she wanted more. But he stopped, as if deciding to leave her wanting. Her eyes trained on his lips, Signey heard the baggage handler close the trunk. "What are you doing, Hawkins?"

"Jess," he reminded her. His fingers dropped to her shoulder, one thumb to her collarbone. "Breaking barriers?"

"Earns you a No Time, hotshot." She knew he'd understand her meaning. Calf ropers were disqualified for breaking the time barrier.

Jess laughed softly, and his smile carried to his eyes and the squint lines around them. His eyes matched the turquoise in his watch.

"A No Time always gets a second chance."

She pushed him away, lest she forget herself all over again. "I'll call if I hear of anything."

"Don't bother. I'll be back."

With his teasing smile and very adept tongue? "You don't have to do that."

"I *want* to. And somehow, blondie, it's about more than Dave." He backed away then, tossed her the keys and blew her a kiss.

She had the crazy urge to duck, then the crazier urge not to. Instead she clutched the little cloisonné hand mirror still in her pocket, and felt instantly soothed.

Like Grandma Jensen's homilies, Signey's little mirror had become her emotional crutch.

JESS SPRANG into the cabin of his plane with a lightheartedness that surprised him. Even though Kelly was four months pregnant and worried sick about Dave, Jess regretted having to betray her confidences to Signey. He had no proof of any wrongdoing . . . yet.

The tower controller interrupted his musings. "Niner-Four-Niner, proceed at will. Watch the thunder boomers over the Bighorn mountain passes." Moments later he was airborne.

What he hadn't expected in all this was that he'd want to see Signey again. Soon. He was committed to the rodeo in Montana, and then he'd planned to spend the next couple of months on his ranch. There was no place on earth as special, as peaceable as the foothills of the Sierra Nevada in high summer.

But now there was Signey Jensen. Blond, strikingly delicate, gritty, caring. Not one woman in a hundred would have responded as she had to his gambit in canceling her flight.

He lived life on the edge and wouldn't have it any other way. He was comfortable with himself. Comfortable with acting on his instincts. He counted on them every hour he spent in the rodeo arena—hours Signey Jensen plainly knew nothing of. She believed he was retired.

Being in Cheyenne for Frontier Days wasn't in his plans. Getting back would be a pain in the carcass. But then, he thought with a smile, a rodeo clown ought to be used to that.

2

FOR THE THIRD TIME in as many days Signey pulled the list of the rodeo contestants from her files. It was no use. She wasn't surprised that Hawkins's name wasn't there, just . . . disappointed. If she had the sense God gave a goose, she'd have been grateful. She understood men like Hawkins—their almost physical need to take risks—but if he came back, it wouldn't be her understanding he was after.

Wyoming, the West, the rodeo arena, everything reminded her of him. Unbidden, Hawkins hovered in her thoughts. Fifty times a day some tiny gesture, some throwaway comment or someone's green eyes summoned Hawkins to her mind. And the flying kiss she hadn't ducked after all. She couldn't remember ever being so distracted. Or so impatient with herself for being that way.

A metallic-blue Jag peeled to a stop outside the rodeo office. Only Kenneth W. Webb would drive the thousands of miles from Atlanta for a one-week gig as her cameraman. The man was as attached to his car as a horse was to its legs.

Bounding into the tiny office provided them by the rodeo committee, Ken promptly plopped into a worn paisley-print armchair. "Hi, sweetstuff. How's it going?"

"Fine—if you'd cut the 'sweetstuff' bit. I know it's asking a lot, Webb, but—"

He held up his hand to forestall her complaints. "Save it, Signeykins. You're the boss. Are you ready to go on over to the arena?"

Signey shook her head. They'd been at this mutilating-her-name routine for years, and he seemed to have every intention of continuing until they were old and gray. She sat on the desk and drew her legs up, settling in.

"I wanted to ask you a question first." She'd been thinking about Dave's suspicions—and about the videotapes. "Didn't you originally work for Finley on the videos for his race cars?"

Ken drew a mechanical pencil from his breast pocket and began rolling it between his fingers. "Yeah. Madigan was Finley's driver then."

"On the track near Searchlight in Nevada?"

"Yep. Why?"

Signey hesitated momentarily. She'd known Dave for seven years. He was California laid-back and appeared as open as a barn door, but he never ran off at the mouth to the wrong people. Never.

"Dave Lindstrom cracked up one of the experimental cars a few days ago."

"No!"

"You hadn't heard?"

"Nothing. Is he okay?"

Signey nodded. "Apparently. I talked to Kelly this morning. Do you know any of the video team at the track now?"

"A few."

"Are they still recording every practice run?"

Ken played the pencil between his fingers and nodded. "I'm sure they'd go over the tapes looking for the reasons he went out of control."

"Is that something Dave would do?"

"Nah. I doubt it. At least Madigan never would have. Why would a driver put himself through it again?"

If he suspected sabotage he would. But though she trusted Ken, Signey couldn't quite voice Dave's suspicions yet. "Do you think Finley would object if, for some reason, Dave did want to see the tape?"

"God, no. He'd want Dave's explanation, I should think. Those cars aren't exactly cheap."

That settled it. If Dave asked for the tape and got it, they could be relatively sure that Finley had nothing to hide. If not—then Dave was very possibly in as much trouble as he feared.

"That's the way to go, then."

Ken pushed off the chair and made for the door. "Well, if that's all you needed, we better get a move on. Don't want to lose the sunset. You ready?"

"Sure," she answered, reaching for her bag. "Only I'm not up to any time trials in your Jag or sweet-talking the local cops out of a speeding ticket."

"No problem. Let's walk over."

"You? Walk?" Lean and athletic looking in his Big Sur way, Ken was unfashionably opposed to physical exercise. Action photography, he claimed, required more than enough of him.

He snorted. "The cops in this one-horse town don't understand me."

"Insufferable snob. I happen to like this *city.*"

"You and fifty thousand other misguided souls."

"You could be covering a golf tourney somewhere," she said, baiting him.

"On the other hand, I kinda enjoyed the barbecue."

For the past few days all they'd done was film preliminary segments on the rodeo: a piece on Cheyenne's history, a short take on the volunteer work involved in producing the Daddy of 'Em All, the barbecue the committeemen had put on for their counterparts from Las Vegas and Oklahoma City. She couldn't blame Ken for wanting to get to the rough-and-tumble action of the competitions. "C'mon," she suggested. "Let's wrap it."

Ken got his equipment while Signey applied fresh lipstick. Clad in close-fitting jeans, an earthen-colored Western shirt and her beloved moccasins, she felt more at home than she'd been in years. She shouldered one of Ken's bags and they walked over to the rodeo arena.

As Ken prepared exactingly for the filming of this segment, she paced the arena, stirring up small clouds of dust. At his signal Signey took her place atop a fence railing. She would do a voice-over as the camera executed a slow pass of the deserted rodeo grounds.

"Go for it, sweetstuff."

Sighing at the defiant repetition of the nickname, Signey matched timing and text cues, then put in her own instructions for the tape editor back in Atlanta. Finally she began her dialogue.

"It's dusk in Cheyenne now on the night before the rodeos begin, and we are on location at the Daddy of 'Em All.

"You can almost feel the history here, the hundred years of men at risk, pitting themselves against a thousand pounds of wild, unbroken horse or the fury of one-ton bulls. You can smell the earth, the sweat and blood of a century of contests, the pungent odor of the stock-yards. You can hear the 'roar of the greasepaint and the smell of the crowds' as rodeo clowns have punned for years.

"Even clowns perform here as bullfighters. They entertain with their antics, but they are, in fact, bullfighters, ready to distract a life-threatening bull from trampling or goring a fallen cowboy. Their clowning is no light responsibility.

"You can sense that this is an arena unlike any other. Here, ominous is more than a word. It's a gut feeling because the conflict between man and beast is so immediate, the challenge powerful and graphic. The stakes are high—the cowboy never goes completely unscathed, and his life may depend on his skill and primal instinct.

"From out of these bucking chutes we will see the rides of the daring, thrill to the excitement of the eight-second clock. Eight seconds is a very, very long time astride a bull.

"I'm Signey Jensen with Cable Sports, and this is Cheyenne Frontier Days, pro rodeo at its outdoor best. Join me tomorrow and every day this week. You'll be glad you did!"

Ken shot Signey a thumbs-up, swung around and lowered the camera from his shoulder. Signey squinted at his profile against the sun descending behind the grandstands.

"Everything copacetic Ken?" she asked, using his favorite slang.

"I don't know about that," came a voice from behind Ken, "but I can smell the blood and guts."

Hawkins. Her pulse quickened quite stupidly. He'd done it again; his entrances were never anything less than staged events. Offering his hand in greeting to Ken, Jess winked at Signey.

"Hi. Jess Hawkins. You must be Signey's crew."

"Yeah. Ken Webb."

"Ken, Jess is Dave Lindstrom's brother-in-law. He's the one who told me about Dave's crash," Signey offered.

"Oh, yeah. Well, so how is Dave?"

Responding to Jess's surprise, Signey explained. "Ken knows the video guys at the practice track, Jess. I trust him. I asked him about the tapes, whether Finley would object to Dave seeing the one of the crash."

Jess nodded, accepting her explanation. "Dave's shaken up, but . . . he's a driver. Maybe a look at the films will help him figure out what went wrong."

"Hope so. It can't be easy to walk away from something like that. Give him my best, will you?"

"Thanks. I'll do that." Jess turned to Signey. "Hi, lady. It's been too long."

"Three days." Such an admission . . . minutes, even seconds were the units she lived by. How many seconds to airtime? How many minutes allotted to this event or that game?

Three days. Four thousand, three hundred and twenty minutes. Signey swallowed.

Ken was speaking again. "Do you two want some film clips for posterity or should I exit, stage left?"

"Exit," Signey directed sternly, but knew her smile ruined the effect. "You have to run the tapes to the airport for counter-to-counter back to Atlanta, anyway."

"Can I borrow your car? The local yokels are threatening to impound my Jag if they catch me on the streets again. I think they're serious this time."

"I'll see you home, Signey," Jess offered.

"I'd appreciate that, if I were going home."

"Anywhere, then. You name it."

"I need to be back in town by eight in the morning," she said, stalling. Was a simple "No, thanks," beyond the abilities of her gilded tongue?

"I have to be up early myself. I'll come get you and you can drop me off in the morning."

Hawkins had an answer for everything. For the moment it seemed more prudent to agree than be outmaneuvered. "Fine, then. That would be fine."

Done packing his gear, Ken crammed Signey's stuff into the shoulder bag she'd carried and beat a hasty retreat. She was alone with Jess.

Hatless, with tawny, tousled hair curling over his open collar, Jess closed the distance between them in a few short, fluid strides.

He draped both forearms over her shoulders. If he knew the gesture was too immediate, too intimate, he didn't show it. His thumb caressed her chin. Perversely, her whole world shrank to the sensation of his touch on her.

"What are you doing here, Hawkins?"

"Looking for you."

"Have you nothing better to do than fly all around the country, looking for me?" The thought was staggering.

"Nope. Do you play poker, Signey?" he asked.

"Some," she admitted.

"Well, flying you home was penny-ante stuff, a little gamble. To get to know you, to see if you could help Dave out." His lips curved into a smile that became a dare. "I'm raising the stakes."

"I'm glad to help. On the other hand, I'm not sure I can afford the kind of stakes you're talking about."

"Dinner? A few hours together?"

"Why do I feel like the deck is stacked when you play poker, Hawkins?"

His smile went crooked. "Why, I'm as honest as the day is long!"

"So much for honesty, then. Hadn't you noticed? This is the end of July and the days are growing shorter and shorter."

Jess laughed and pleasure lit his features. "Are we on, then?"

"Actually I do need to put in an appearance at the mayor's reception. There are going to be a lot of people there I need to connect with. And then I'm supposed to meet Max Blane in the morning for my bullfighter interviews." *Why* was she babbling on, making excuses, wavering like prairie grasses in the breeze? "I need to go over my notes for that, and—"

Jess put a finger to her lips, hushing her. "I'm crowding you."

"A little," she agreed. Was he going to protect her from himself?

"I didn't come back only because I wanted to take you to dinner, Signey. I'm thirty-six years old, babe, and used to coming after what I want."

Babe. How was it possible that he could make her wish for all the things she would never accept from another man? *Babe*, for instance. He was off-limits to her.

A rakehell, danger-courting man like Hawkins would *always* be off-limits to her.

"Did you think I needed a warning?" she chided.

Jess laughed. The woman needed a warning real bad. The thought of touching her again had made him edgy for three days. An eternity. "Yeah, I do. And I think maybe you're scared."

Her long brown lashes fluttered against the flush on her cheeks. Touching her, only touching, wouldn't do. He bent to taste her, and a tiny sound of strangled pleasure escaped her when his lips skimmed lightly over hers with the promise of a kiss. The sound, the texture of her lips drew him like a moth to a flame.

He drew her nearer. The warmth of his breath touched her lips. He was right. She was scared. But his touch trailed wild shivers up her arms until he cupped her head and her hands came to rest upon his hips.

The shouts of gathering cowboys and the grounds crew reminded Jess where he was. A rodeo arena was no place to take a woman. He had other plans, other sensual games to play with her besides upping the ante.

"C'mon, Signey Jensen. Let's go to your reception and be scared as hell together."

Throughout the reception, Signey fought to still the thrumming of her heart and the insistent tug of crazy desires. Her throat grew so dry it hurt.

"Will you make yourself useful and introduce me around?"

"Sure. And you'll feed me afterward."

"Afterward I have to go home and review for—"

He interrupted. "I know, I know. Your bullfighter interview. One step at a time, babe."

One step at a time. Her heart was bounding ahead of her. Way ahead of her. *Babe.*

Suddenly she wanted what she'd never have dreamed of accepting from another man.

HOURS AFTER they'd arrived at the Hitching Post, both ballrooms were wall-to-wall with rodeo fans. When the blaring country and western band began to croon something silly about getting drop-kicked through life's goalposts, Jess looked at Signey with a humorous, defeated expression and jerked his head in the direction of the doors.

"Any chance we could get out of here soon?" he shouted over the raucous music.

"Every chance." Signey said. "I'll never find anybody in this crowd." She was tired of searching among all the friendly confusion and milling bodies and began threading her way out, with Jess right behind her. When they got to his rental car, he helped her into the passenger seat and took the wheel.

"Alone, at last." He stroked her neck in idle, sensual circles.

Signey swallowed, forcing back feelings she hadn't experienced with such speed in a very long time. She met his eyes, glittering in the darkness and silence, and knew she didn't want him to stop toying with her hair. "I'd already forgotten what it was like to be one-on-one with you."

"What's it like, Signey?" His voice was throaty.

"Claustrophobic," she quipped, but the truth wouldn't go unsaid. "And if I were truly honest—" his thumb was at her lower lip "—very, very nice."

"Nice," he repeated.

"Very nice," she corrected him. Like the rough texture of his thumb, tracing her lip. Like his smile. Maybe sexy, and not nice at all.

"Where did you go, babe, when you were in high school and wanted to neck?"

"They've built a shopping mall there."

He relented. "Okay. Where do the natives go to eat?"

Signey laughed. "I haven't been here in years, but *this* native used to go home."

"Is that an invitation? I could really go for a fried-egg sandwich or two and a beer."

"All right. But my dad never allowed necking on the couch."

Jess smiled crookedly. "A virgin sofa? Interesting possibilities."

"It wasn't meant to be a challenge, Hawkins." Would she have the wits left to fry eggs?

"Yeah, but there's not much I don't take that way." All the same, he straightened in his seat, took his arm from around her and started the car.

He drove following her directions, carrying on a conversation about the time he'd been in Cheyenne and dislocated a shoulder saddling a horse. By the time he pulled into the circle driveway of her family's two-story, Signey had begun to relax.

Jess got out, helped Signey, then put one arm casually over her shoulder. "Where's the tree with your swing?"

"Over there." Signey gestured. "But the swing is gone."

"Too bad. Bet your dad never thought to outlaw necking on the swing."

Signey elbowed him not too gently in the ribs. "What my dad never knew never hurt him."

Jess felt a curious stab of envy. "So you did neck in the swing?"

"Never. But only because I didn't think of it. So what do you think?"

He thought he was real glad she'd never been in her swing with some jerk, but obliged her by looking around. "Not much to see in the moonlight. How big is the spread?"

"As far as you can see, in the daylight. Too big. My father liked to hang around with the ranching crowd— he hit every rodeo from here to Texas, but he only leased out the land for grazing for a few years to a guy who ran a calf-breeding operation."

"Seems a waste. So what does he do?"

Signey separated from Jess to reach into her purse for her house keys. "He's a stockbroker. But . . . well, you know. Land is a very powerful symbol of money in the West."

The living room boasted wing chairs, glass tables, a ten-foot, emerald-green sofa and Baccarat crystal in an elegant liquor cabinet.

Jess was drawn to the wall of skiing awards—trophies, plaques, photos—that had belonged to her brother. Signey had long since stopped noticing them, but now they seemed even more ostentatious than the display of her parents' wealth.

"Paul Jensen," he said. "Your . . . ?"

"Brother," she supplied. Signey stepped to Jess's left and pointed to a picture of Paul at the US trials for the Olympics in Grenoble. "He was killed after this was taken."

"I remember hearing about that. I'm sorry."

"Save your sympathy, Jess. It happened a long time ago." Turning on her heel, she led the way to the kitchen.

Jess took over the cooking as soon as Signey had pulled the eggs and butter from the refrigerator. "So. How come your pictures and things aren't up?"

Signey opened a bottle of beer for each of them and sat down at the table. "If you feel a cliché coming on, Hawkins, kindly stifle it."

Jess served up his eggs, dumped catsup onto them and closed his sandwiches. "What cliché would that be?"

"Sibling lives in her big brother's shadow." *Or, parents barely noticed they had a second child.*

"Did you?"

"Live in Paul's shadow? Probably."

Jess wasn't fooled. It took a clown to recognize one, and he knew her smile glossed over old hurts he was unaccountably anxious to soothe. "And afterward?"

Signey picked at the label on the beer bottle with her thumbnail. "I was eleven when Paul died. I was there, Jess. I saw him take the ski jump, saw him go out of control. Saw him crash into a tree.... Afterward I discovered that I was on my own—emotionally." Pieces of the label flaked off. "But that was a long time ago, Jess. A very long time. Does that explain things?"

Jess thought he'd probably heard more than she'd ever revealed before. Soothing old hurts wasn't a one-time deal, and he didn't know if he'd be around to ease them forever. Oddly, he began to think about that possibility. About loving her till old hurts were only distant memories. "Yeah, Signey. That explains it fine."

"Good." She sat back, smiling. "So tell me. What kind of big brother were you to Kelly?"

Jess leaned back and smiled as well. "I was always double-daring her into doing the things I wanted to do. She was hell on wheels, though. Right from the first. Rodeo was my only hope."

Signey sipped from her bottle of beer, amused. "How?"

"I started riding the unbroken ranch stock to prove there was at least one thing I could do that Kelly couldn't. 'Course, if I'd have let up on her just a little, I wouldn't have had to go to such extremes."

"Liar. I know your kind. A thrill a minute, nothing less will do."

Which was precisely why it bordered on insanity to have brought him home, Signey thought. A man like Jess flirted with disaster every day. She'd seen her brother die in a horrible, deadly accident, and she would never lose her heart to someone who lived life on that kind of razor's edge.

Jess tipped his beer bottle in Signey's direction in a kind of salute. "Kelly would never let me get by with blaming it all on her, either."

His eyes swept over her and Signey's breathing failed once again. That look that made her feel so special. "Hawkins?" Using his last name to foil intimacy was getting to be a habit—that and changing the subject. "I spoke to Kelly on the phone this morning. She didn't sound well at all."

Jess picked up his third sandwich. "She's a trouper, Signey, but she's looking a little pale to me. Besides which, the twins are getting to be a handful, and Jason is just a year old."

Signey nodded. The twins, a five-year-old boy and girl, had been a handful from birth. "Is there anything physically wrong with Kelly?"

"Her doctor says no. Her blood counts are okay and she didn't have any trouble with the twins or Jason. But you know Kel. She's always been nonchalant as hell about Dave's close calls. Since we talked, she seems . . . brittle, I guess. You know what I mean?"

Signey did. Brittle was a reaction she understood very well. Too well. "I'm really hopeful about the practice-run videotapes. If Finley has no problem letting Dave see them, that would pretty well rule him out as culpable."

"Tell me more about Ken Webb. I take it you didn't tell him Dave is running scared."

"When I first met Ken Webb, he'd just come to Atlanta from the track in Searchlight. He still knows a few guys there, if we need to talk to somebody."

"Does Dave know Webb?"

"No. Dave came after Madigan retired from the racing circuit."

Jess worried a toothpick between his lips. "Finley has a real history of overextending himself. Maybe his little house of cards is finally coming down. The newer, experimental cars must be taking one hell of a bite out of the old pocket. Do you think Ken will help if it comes to that?"

"Yes, I do. Ken is . . . hopeless. A terrible womanizer, but he has a heart as big as outdoors. Finley isn't his favorite person in the whole world, either."

Without taking his eyes from Signey's, Jess slugged down the rest of his beer. "Sounds like you know him pretty well."

"He's the best camera jockey I've ever worked with."

Jess's tilted chair fell back with a thud, and he got up to rinse his dishes in the sink. "C'mon," he urged, offering his hand. "We'll find a way to avoid the virgin sofa and I'll tell you a story."

They wandered through the darkened house hand in hand and passed the sofa as Jess had promised. The swing hanging from the eaves on the front porch was nearly as dangerous, but they sat down there, nonetheless, Signey on one side, Jess on the other. Jess pulled off his boots and made himself comfortable. Signey waited and stared at the quarter moon and starlit landscape, listening to the calls of crickets in the night.

"You're planning a segment on bullfighters—the rodeo clowns?" he inquired at last.

Signey nodded. "I've got it all arranged with Max Blane. His contract came in while I was making arrangements, and he agreed to do it for me."

"Max isn't coming to Cheyenne."

"He *what?* I've arranged an entire segment around him!" Hawkins's expression roused her suspicions. "What's going on, Jess?"

"I paid him off. That's my ace in the hole. I wanted to come back to Cheyenne. Frankly, it's the freckle." He reached out to touch her earlobe. "I'm replacing him for whatever you had in mind." And the things *he* had in mind as well.

Jess, a bullfighter! Surprise flared in her. He'd said he wasn't competing anymore.

She should have known better. Panic seized her because he made her feel special and womanly, and she'd already begun to care for him. "You? You're bullfighting?"

"Yeah. Not in competition, but for the bull riders."

"But Max—?"

"Max was a real sport. He guessed right off."

"Guessed what?"

"That I was out to impress some hometown woman. I was offered the clowning contract in the first place, but turned it down. Why else buy off a contract I hadn't bid on in the first place? I didn't bother explaining that this woman was different."

His thumbs caressed the tender, vulnerable flesh on the insides of her wrists. His eyes searched hers for a reaction. He wanted her to be pleased that he'd gone to such trouble.

She was.

Signey felt the thrumming beat of her heart at her throat, the tensing anticipation of her shoulders as his fingers made their way up her arms.

He moved nearer, until only her jeans and his cords separated them. He cupped her chin in his fingers and drew it aside so that his lips grazed her jaw, ending at the lobe of her ear.

Signey closed her eyes. An ache settled deep, deep within her and Jess's throaty voice encouraged it. His lips brushed her ear.

"Believe it, Signey. I want you." Then he kissed her, not as before, teasing and light, but long and hard. The response in her matched his, need for need, hunger for hunger, rattling her badly. "Jess, no."

"Jess, yes." A tiny stroke of his tongue against her earlobe reduced her to jelly. "More rhyme." His fingers threaded through her hair; his hands cupped each side of her head. His eyes glittered with humor and passion. The combination unnerved her. "And...more reason."

Rhyme? Reason? His touch rekindled embers she had thought well scattered, and she couldn't think or stop her arms from encircling his neck, her fingers from threading themselves into his hair, pulling him closer still.

"It may rhyme, Hawkins, but it makes no sense at all." He was a bullfighter. He faced a ton of killing animal flesh every time he walked into a rodeo arena. She couldn't live with that.

"Jess I... I just can't. I think you'd better go now. And don't worry about picking me up in the morning. I'll have Ken drive out."

Brittle. He'd seen it in Kelly's eyes and he recognized it now. "The hell you will."

"Jess, you don't really know me. You may think you do, but you don't."

He pulled back a little, leaning into the pillows of the swing, watching her too closely for comfort. "What should I know, Signey?"

"I could care for you, Jess, but—"

"It's the haircut, isn't it?" he teased, ramming a hand through his hair. "I could get it—"

"This isn't a joke, Hawkins. Not everything is a joke. I don't have what it takes to pick up the pieces when you go down."

"Faulty logic, babe. I don't intend to go down, fall down or lie down. Except..." He grinned. "Well, maybe *lie* down."

Signey landed an only half-playful punch to his shoulder. "Logic has nothing to do with it. I'm entitled to feelings, Hawkins, just like anybody else."

Jess pulled on his boots again and kissed her. A gentle, light touch of his lips to hers. "People get killed crossing the street, Signey. People get killed in plane crashes. Have you thought of that?"

"Yes, but you—"

"Wait and see, okay? Most of the time bullfighting is just boring as hell."

"Grandma Jensen warned me about men like you."

"Did she?" Jess smirked.

"Yes. 'Boys will say anything, Signey Marie,' she'd say. 'Anything to get their way with you.'" Signey wanted almost to cry. "Don't try and kid a kidder, Jess. I've been around the block a few times, and I know you aren't in that arena every day because bullfighting is boring."

"But you don't know how good I am." With another quick kiss and caress of her hair, he was up and gone, leaving her to wonder. "Tomorrow, Signey."

Jess just didn't know, couldn't know. How good he was was no comfort to her. No comfort at all. Signey went inside, in search of her hand mirror, the one her brother had given her more than twenty years ago.

See, Sis, it's a mirror, and when you look into it, it's impossible to cry.

Her big brother's impatient strategy had worked then and it worked now. Signey didn't cry anymore.

3

"BY TIME-HONORED tradition, the rodeo bullfighters dress as clowns. Their costumes serve two purposes. The bright colors attract the attention of the bulls, enabling the bullfighting clown to distract them from injuring fallen cowboys. Beyond that, the clowns entertain the spectators with their antics."

Cuing Ken to focus on Jess, Signey described his costume as the afternoon's rodeo announcer introduced Jess and his fellow clowns.

"Jess Hawkins is the primary bull fighter. Even though his face is not grease-painted like the others, he's having a good time out there, wheeling and turning and bucking on a child's stick horse."

He wore a red-and-white-striped shirt, a pink paisley scarf around his neck, heart-embellished suspenders and cutoff overalls over red tights. His baseball spikes provided traction and speed. As the announcer noted the substitution for Max Blane, Jess drew himself up in a mock salute, removed his hat and swept the arena dirt in a low bow. The crowd roared its approval, then echoed itself for the parade of Oglala Sioux Indians in full regalia.

Signey watched as Ken carried out her instructions, panning the arena and the shambles of cowboys lining the fences. "Keep an eye on the clowns, Ken. They should be pulling a stunt soon."

Climbing over a railing, she took her place above the bucking chutes and switched her mike to Recording. She described the feeling of expectancy that permeated the air like the dust from the arena.

After the national anthem one of Jess's cohorts set off an oversize cannon. A tiny brindled fluff of a dog came scurrying out of the paisley wad everyone had thought they'd seen bursting from the cannon. The little dog leaped into the clown's overalls and two geese scrambled out his pant legs. The show was on.

"Okay, Ken, let's focus on the chutes." They'd agreed earlier to concentrate on the bucking chutes where the contestants riding wild broncs and Brahman bulls erupted into action.

Jess stood ready, shading his eyes against the sun as he looked up to where Signey sat. Only a few yards separated them. He winked broadly and Signey smiled, then carefully switched her recording equipment so that the rodeo announcer's words could be taped directly from his microphone.

"First out of the chutes this afternoon will be Marty McCabe of Albuquerque, New Mexico." The announcer described the Brangus bull under McCabe, then explained that the cowboy was a rookie who had just earned an official PRCA permit. "I can tell you there ain't a bull rider around that's not grittin' his teeth, gettin' down on an animal that size."

Signey checked Ken's position in the arena. Well out of harm's way, he made full use of his state-of-the-art zoom lens equipment.

The announcer continued his narration, filling the moments until the cowboy nodded his readiness. When he did, the excitement in the announcer's voice increased. Signey's heart began skipping beats.

The bull was a disappointment. The young cowboy rode to the count, hopped off and out of the way. The animal just wasn't interested. Jess and a cohort drew the bull farther into the arena. The animal charged once, then stopped dead in his tracks. Jess swatted him with his hat, and another clown pulled his tail.

Switching the recording equipment back to her mike, Signey resumed speaking. "The crowd loves it. They're shouting advice to the clowns." Her eyes riveted on Jess, she continued. "This bull was no challenge at all. You can see Jess Hawkins signaling to the hazers to shoo the bull out of the arena."

The next five cowboys were thrown seconds ahead of the whistle blast, and Jess moved with a lanky, bored stride to the bucking chutes, kneeling to await the next go-around of bull riding.

Finally the third heat approached. Ken climbed a fence to get a close-up of the cowboy mounting the bull he'd drawn, and Signey described the qualities a bull-fighting clown had to possess.

"These men need a combination of split-second timing, perfect nerves, courage and..." She hesitated as the announcer introduced the next rider; the chute gate was jerked open. Signey shot to her feet along with every spectator in the crowd.

The bull fired out. The cowboy was already in trouble. Signey forced herself to continue. "It's a cyclone of a bull! You can see Hawkins and his partner moving in. The boy's off balance...farther and farther out... He's down! The bull's turning back, eyeing the cowboy... He's, oh God, he's in trouble! No, wait.... Hawkins is there...." Hawkins. The man she refused to worry about.

Suddenly caught between the snorting, furious bull and the madly scrambling cowboy, Jess heaved the youngster aside, somehow distracting the huge, cunning beast, battering at him with a Frisbee. Now Jess was in danger....

"Hawkins's partner is there. He's trying to pull the bull's attention away." Her voice cracked with strain. "No way. The animal's not about to be distracted." *Move, Jess, for God's sake, move!* she wanted to scream.

"Hawkins has hit the ground. Better to be trampled than gored. He's crawling out from underneath." Jess literally rolled out and leaped to his feet, out of danger.

The bull wasn't finished yet, but Jess had escaped a stomping. He made for the barrel and his partner jumped inside it. Confused now by the disappearance of Jess's partner, the bull lowered its head. The creature bawled out its frustration, mauling the loose dirt with its front hooves.

"It's at a charging run now, but Hawkins is working the barrel. It's a beautiful job. Watch how he keeps that barrel between himself and the bull."

Jess. The admiration in her words had been purely professional. The worry was all woman.

Jess was a bullfighter. He'd told her that, but hearing it and seeing him at it were two very different things. A bullfighter, and Signey had begun to fall. Hard.

JESS CROUCHED behind the open-ended barrel, facing down the critter that'd given him the first real chal-

lenge in more than a month. Saliva hung in strands
from the jaws of the bull; its rangy sides heaved from
the exertion. Jess noted all of that and none of it. He
sensed rather than saw the fight drawing to a close. The
beast would give up first.

Still he glared into its raging, confused eyes. Power,
certainty and satisfaction sang in Jess. He clenched his
fists in a subconscious gesture of victory. Ken caught it
all, distracting Jess for a fraction of a heartbeat by his
presence a couple of yards away. Out here Jess measured time by his own heartbeat.

Then he remembered his role, the clowning, the
crowd of clamoring fans. *His* crowd. His fellow clown
crawled out of the barrel when the bull swung its mas-
sive head in the other direction. Jess casually spun the
huge, rolling prop, then jumped onto the barrel with a
catlike bound and began walking it away from the bull
like a lumberjack rolling a log. He mimed a march until the crowd began clapping in Sousa time, then took
a diving bow off the barrel. Another day, another dollar.

Like hell. Another day, another thrill, another high
he would never get tired of. He looked for Signey. Some
primal, admittedly macho instinct made him crave a
look of admiration from her for his feats. The crowd no
longer mattered. Signey was nowhere to be seen. Sharp
disappointment sniped from within.

He kicked at the arena dust, flung his battered, horn-
pierced hat at the bull the hazers had finally headed toward the gates and left the arena. Ducking into the on-
site trailer, he stripped out of his clowning duds and
hauled on a pair of Levi's. Picking up his straw Stetson, he went looking for Signey.

What he'd expected, he didn't know, but Signey kneeling at the feet of a young cowboy, wrapping an ankle wasn't it. From a distance of fifty paces Jess could see the youngster hovering between tears for the pain and tears for the treat of feminine attention.

Equally torn, Jess wandered within listening distance and leaned against a barn door. Signey had told him she couldn't be there to pick up the pieces if he went down. Well, damn it, he hadn't gone down. Fact was, he'd had one hell of a day and wanted her to appreciate the fact, but here she was, picking up pieces instead. Someone else's pieces.

"Ma'am," the kid said, "I just gotta get back out there."

"I'm almost done," Signey soothed. "Does that feel like it's going to support your ankle?"

"Yeah. Ain't you gonna ask me why?"

Signey smiled at the boy and shook her head. Dust and hay strands made her strawberry-blond hair look as if she'd taken a tumble in a haystack. Angry though he was, the image pleased Jess.

"No," she said. "Should I?"

"Well, you're a reporter, ain't you?"

"Yeah. But not your mother. You don't have to tell me. I know why."

"You do?"

"Lonnie, you've gone pro rodeo. You have a job to do, bucks to bring home, your self-respect to live up to." Signey paused, mustering the strength and leverage to wind the last length of the Ace bandage as tightly as she could. She finished it off, binding it in as well as any doctor Jess had ever seen. "Those are some pretty darn good reasons for getting back out there."

Disgust overcame the grimace on the boy's painfully young face. "Shoot. I ain't made more'n traveling money yet." He thumped angrily at the rim of a Stetson imitation.

Jess had never been where this kid was now—so broke that it wasn't the next meal he wondered about so much as the next ride and the hope of a fat purse to repay the last meal. But he knew the story too well. A hundred, a thousand like the boy came and went every year. Broke and busted up. In body and spirit as much as in the pocket.

Signey obviously understood it, too, and that pleased Jess a lot.

"It's in your bones. Go to it, cowboy. Give 'em hell," she said encouragingly.

Jess ambled toward them, unable to stay away any longer. "See to it, Lonnie. Wouldn't want to disappoint the lady." Jess let his knee brush her shoulder. When he got right down to the truth, he was less angry than disappointed that Signey refused to hang around and be impressed by him; now *he* wanted her attention.

Though she said nothing, he sensed the change in her, the softening, the anticipation, the awareness of him. The young cowboy eased himself up against the back of the barn, wide-eyed as he recognized Jess, and eager again in spite of the obvious pain.

"No, siree. Hey. Thanks a bunch. Both of ya." He hobbled off, renewed and anxious for another fracas, the one that might yield up a few bucks.

Signey rose, watching the cowboy go. The July sun shone upon her hair. Here behind the barns a few rodeo hands moved tiredly about. The noise of the crowd followed the crescendo of the announcer's voice as some bulldogger wrestled a steer to the ground in under five seconds—the best time of the show. Jess watched Signey watching her conquest limp away.

He'd turn back every so often and each time Signey waved. The gesture made the fabric of her shirt tighten against her slender back. Jess began measuring time in heartbeats again.

"I could kill," he murmured.

Signey turned slowly and brought up her hand to shade her eyes against the glaring sun. Time beat a little faster.

"Jealous?" she teased. "It shows."

"Makes me wish I'd missed a step out there."

"You were . . . incredible out there." They stood toe to toe. Sweat and grime and power clung to him. Especially power.

He touched her cheek. "You were incredible, babe, with that kid. He needed your pep talk worse than he needed his ankle wrapped."

Together they walked toward the park, away from the rodeo grounds. Her hip brushed his leg every other step. Casually Jess hooked a finger through a belt loop on the back of her jeans. If he touched her, he'd have had to find a way, a place to take her there and then.

Jess cleared his throat. "Are you done for the day?"

"Yeah. You?"

"Yeah. Want to go make some splendor in the grass?"

Signey struggled vainly against the smile breaking on her lips and shook her head. "Trite, Hawkins. Can't keep up that famous breakneck pace, huh?"

He stopped short and pulled her up against a tree with him. His fingers clung to her belt loop; his arm encircled her. He could trade lusty, rapid-fire witticisms with her from now till Christmas, but he had never had so much *else* to say to a woman. Or found so few ways to say them. "Is my tongue tied in a knot, d'you think?"

She toyed with the open placket of his shirt. "Would it be too indelicate of me to hope that it's not?"

"Oh, God," he breathed. His flesh slammed into the bindings of button-fly jeans, and he knew he was in trouble. He hauled her closer still and sank his lips to her hair, warm and redolent of hyacinths and hay. He could hold her here like this until a more subtle moon replaced the glaring sun.

She clung to his shirt and let herself lean into him, struggling with the knowledge that she'd fallen for him. Less than an hour ago he'd stood alone against a ton of angry animal, defying the odds. Defying death. But Signey felt the rigid length of him pressed to her belly, and the part of her that coveted that fulfillment scattered her fears like the fuzzy spikelets of a late-spring dandelion. Only overpowering feelings were left. Sensation. Greed. Her eyes fluttered and closed.

Jess held her to him, his own eyes closed, too, and let himself go with just that pleasure. She fitted to his body like no woman ever had. Her head nestled against the upper slope of his pectorals, in the slight hollow beneath his collarbone. He could rest his cheek on the top of her head and feel her hair catching on whiskers not half a day old.

And if he still recalled the betrayal of Signey's picking up the kid cowboy's pieces when she'd promised she wouldn't do that for him, he told himself that the kid was back in the arena and he was here, holding her.

He'd wanted her to appreciate his skill; at the moment he wanted nothing more than the feel of her sweet, rounded breasts flattened against his ribs.

If they heard Ken approach or call out, not once but three times, they gave no indication. From ten feet away he cleared his throat loudly. Jess noticed first, and the change in the way he held her cued Signey to the fact that they weren't alone. They pulled apart, and Signey turned to look back. Threatened by a wave of awkwardness, she picked up on Ken's distress the instant she quit worrying about what he thought of her being in Jess's arms.

"What is it, Ken? What's happened?"

"It's Dave, Jess. There's been another accident on the track in Nevada." He held up a hand to head off the obvious question. "He walked away from it again."

"Are you kidding me? I didn't even know he planned to be back in Vegas so soon."

"No kidding, Jess. Your mother called the rodeo office. Dave and Kelly got in this morning, and Dave went out to the track. Your mom said Dave's okay, but Kelly's scared bad. Guess they thought she'd miscarry after the accident. She's battling it out in the hospital."

"The baby?" Signey wanted to know.

Ken shrugged. "They don't know yet. Your mom said she'd sure like it if you could come back, overnight at least."

"Let's go, Jess," Signey urged. "There's something going on."

"I'll go. But can you leave? Your assignment here is—"

"It'll keep. I'm going with you, Jess. Dave and Kelly mean too much to me to sit around here."

"Would you guys mind if I tag along?" Ken inquired. "Chances are a lot higher I'll hear something over a beer than long-distance."

Jess nodded. "I'd appreciate that, Ken. How soon can you pack a bag?"

JESS LANDED THE BONANZA at McCarran International Airport at precisely eight-thirty. If it had been hot in Cheyenne, it was blistering in Las Vegas. Steeping the desert landscape in shades of mauve and scarlet, even the twilight did nothing to cool the one hundred-plus temperature. Washing over Signey in waves, the heat equaled her rising concern.

At her insistence, Jess rented two cars. It was vital that she and Ken get to the scene of the crash before any more time passed. And just as vital that Kelly get some support from Jess.

"I wish you'd wait till I can come with you," he protested. Fact was, he didn't want her to go off hell-bent for trouble.

Signey couldn't prevent herself smoothing the polished cotton shirt over Jess's chest. The last time anyone had worried over her, she'd been in braces. His protectiveness felt strangely cluttered with unspoken man-woman declarations, and it would have been so easy to give in to him and wait.

She knew that if Walter Finley had anything to do with Dave's accidents, her presence would threaten him in ways that could spell the end of her career at Cable Sports. And even if Dave had the proverbial nine lives of a cat, he had precious few left. Yet no matter what it meant to her job, she couldn't ignore something as improbable as a second crash in less than two weeks.

Pretending a lot more moxie than she felt, Signey sent Jess on his way. "Kelly and Dave need you, now. And your mom."

McCarran Airport sat on the south side of town. While Jess headed the Honda Prelude north to Flamingo, Signey directed Ken in their minivan to the highway then south toward the little town called Searchlight. Dave's home track was built on the salt flats nearby.

Hours after the crash, a cleanup crew of a dozen or more was still dragging pieces of wreckage away. The local press had come out in full force—yet for all that, there wasn't a camera to be seen. Not even the Finley video equipment.

"Better leave your camera in the trunk, Ken. For now."

Ken reached out to stay her hand. "Are you sure, Signey? If Finley finds out you're here, you could be history."

Ken's concern only served to carve her resolve in granite. They got out of the car and mingled among the crowd. It was quiet. Too quiet.

"Bad news travels fast, I guess." Signey nodded to a casual competitor from another network, but Ken took her arm and guided her away.

"If these jackals realize you're here, they'll all think you, as Cable Sports, have a leg up on them. They wouldn't be hanging around if they'd got what they came for."

Signey and Ken paced around the edges of the activity. From the looks of the wreck, it had been another minor miracle that Dave had survived at all, much less walked away from it. They followed a trail of burned rubber, skirted the accident site itself and walked on, talking over the possibilities.

"Maybe I could get to someone on the pit crew, Ken, and you could look for the video—"

She stopped, startled out of her plan to split up. Against the perimeter wall lay Dave's personalized, jet-black crash helmet. She looked behind them and around, then strolled over to the helmet and picked it up. The vent port was broken up, but the shiny, Formica-like surface of the shell, though scarred, was intact.

"He threw it, Ken. He pulled it off and bashed it against the wall." Dave's temper was as explosive as his driving, but she knew it took more than bad luck to trigger this kind of blind fury in her friend.

"Hey! You! What do you think you're doing!" Uttering a string of foul language, a knot of threatening men—Dave's pit crew or a cleanup team?—roiled toward them. Ken tried to move in front of her, but Signey shoved Dave's crash helmet at him and darted forward.

"Picking up the pieces. What are you doing?"

"You pick yourself up and get the hell outa here, lady. Both of you."

"When I find out why Dave's car crashed again, I will." Her hands shook. She jammed her fingers into the back pockets of her jeans and stood her ground. "Not one minute before."

"Lady," the pack leader intoned crudely, "you see that rope over there? And all the press waiting behind it? When we figure it out, we'll let you know, but since that's like as not weeks from now—"

"Why? Why weeks from now? Why isn't anybody taking pictures?" Gesturing at the carefully placed poles where the videotape cameras should have been, Signey bullied right back, "And why did Dave bash his helmet into the wall?"

The small crowd of press members pushed past the rope barrier to them. The thug type threatening Signey looked nervously around and glared at her.

"The guy's been an accident lookin' for a place to happen for weeks. A basket case. He's wiped out over seven hundred and fifty grand here, and if Finley wants to keep—"

"Excuse me." The crowd stood aside for a feral-faced man in a Brooks Brothers suit and Italian shoes. A Rolex encircled his wrist, and he wore a pinky ring set with an emerald the size of Nevada. Behind him stood Walter Finley, sports mogul, owner of the track and Signey's boss.

"I don't believe I've had the pleasure, Miss?"

"Jensen. Signey Jensen." Her fellow press members reached for notepads. The crowd grew excited; the evening might not be a wash, after all. She looked straight at Walter Finley and was shocked by his beleaguered, almost haggard appearance. Men like him had the time and money never to look so stressed. He, too, was dressed expensively, but Finley appeared rumpled.

Signey turned to the man who had addressed her. "And you are?"

"Phillip Mancouso, Miss Jensen. Corporate attorney, Finley West. I understood you to be safely tucked away in Wyoming, assigned to cover some . . . rodeo." He might as well have said "a jacks' tournament."

"Do you keep track of *all* the little people in Finley's fiefdom?"

"No, Ms. Jensen," Finley interrupted coldly, "he doesn't. Only the ones who can't remember which side their bread is buttered on."

"I'm on my own time. I got here and I'll get back. But first I intend to get—"

"You'll get nothing, Ms. Jensen, but a great deal of grief for your trouble. Do I make myself clear?"

The reporters jockeyed for better positions. Ken tugged at her elbow. "Come on, Signey. It isn't worth it."

"Wait a minute." For a moment her daring flagged. Was there any point in aggravating Finley or his big-gun attorney? She had a feeling that it might already be too late. If Finley had his way, the official story would put the blame upon Dave, no matter what the truth.

She'd known Dave Lindstrom too long and too well to believe that he'd suddenly become a nervous driver, a basket case. Two unlikely accidents were one too many to chalk up to chance. She pulled her last ace out of the hole and thought of Jess, of poker and of stakes she couldn't afford.

"Are you saying that the rest of the press can hang around? That your own network won't cover the crash of one of your cars?"

Finley swore and started threateningly toward her. Mancouso put out a hand to stop him. It worked. Barely.

"Look, Ms. Jensen," he said smoothly. "What Mr. Finley is trying to say is that there is no story here."

"Then I'm officially asking on Dave's behalf for copies of the videotapes from these accidents."

By now Finley seemed to have recovered a measure of composure. "Jensen, don't make me laugh. Even if there were anything—and there's nothing, not one damn thing—to see on those tapes, they belong to me."

"If there's nothing to see, Mr. Finley, then there should be nothing to fear. No reason not to let Dave see them!"

Mancouso stepped in front of Finley and looked pointedly at the crowd of her peers standing around them. "Ms. Jensen, I'm asking you nicely, now. Drop this whole thing and go home. You're too emotionally involved to cover anything to do with Dave Lindstrom. If I'm not wrong, he's a friend of yours—isn't that right?—a close, *personal* friend."

Mancouso paused for effect and got the desired result. From the expressions on the faces of her colleagues, she knew he'd managed to hang her.

Signey bit back a denial that could only reinforce Mancouso's claim, and the crowd began to break up. With one masterly shot from Finley's big gun her credibility was ruined.

AN HOUR LATER, Signey stood in front of the hospital where Kelly had been taken, taping a correspondent file with Ken for counter-to-counter service back to the Atlanta headquarters.

A second accident near Searchlight, Nevada, occurred on the Finley test track this afternoon. Dave Lindstrom was again the driver of the experimental car, which sources at the track estimated to be worth over seven hundred and fifty thousand dollars. As with the crash a few weeks ago, Lind-

strom walked away from it, badly shaken but un-
hurt.

This is Sunrise Hospital on Maryland Parkway,
several blocks east of the famed Las Vegas Strip.
Lindstrom is here, not for overnight observation,
but because his wife, Kelly, who is pregnant, went
into shock upon hearing of the second crash. It
appears that Kelly and her unborn baby have come
through the worst of it.

Authorities in the . . . Phillip Mancouso at . . .
Officials at the track assure us . . .

Ken lowered the videocam from his shoulder. "Signey? I thought you weren't going to mention Mancouso."

"I wasn't," she snapped. "But this is the biggest pack
of lies and evasions. . . . I can't do it, Ken. Every other
network is going to hit on Dave's mental state, and Finley cries foul. I won't do it."

"Do it, Signey."

Jess. She whirled around, and her notepad sailed
across the space between them. Jess sauntered up, bent
to retrieve it and handed it back to her.

"Cut the human interest in Kelly and do it," he said
again.

"Jess . . . I . . . it'll finish him. He'll never find another
group of backers, not in a million years. Why?"

"It's over anyway, babe."

"It's a far cry from over! Those bastards—"

"Have tried twice to get rid of him. They won't blow
it again, Signey." For the space of a heartbeat he stroked
her chin. His hand curved around to the back of her

neck and massaged the knots of tension and anger. Smoky, gentle green eyes bade her to trust him.

"What did he tell you?"

"They're out to get him, Signey. He's survived two accidents. Neither of you can accuse Finley without proof."

"Then I just won't report the story!"

"You've got to, babe. You have to make Finley and everyone else believe that you've accepted their version."

"That Dave's lost his nerve? Or what? They'll try again?"

"Yeah, Signey. They might." Jess raked his fingers over the knot of tension in his own neck.

Tremors of rage and uncertainty rocked her. She had never despised anyone in her life as much as she did Finley and his lawyer at that moment. Dave's career was over if Jess was right.

"Why, Jess? What's he done that's so threatening to them?"

"Dave says Finley has been trimming the research and development money. Rumor has it that there will be no more development, no new cars. According to some kid on the pit crew, they're all looking for new jobs—which tells Dave that Finley must be in deep financial straits. Of course, Finley has no idea what proof Dave has dredged up, but at the moment Finley has the consortium of backers in his hip pocket, and he can't afford to lose them."

Signey's teeth closed over her lower lip. Undoubtedly Jess was right. It looked as though Dave's suspicions had threatened Finley to the point where he'd somehow sabotaged his own cars in an attempt to kill

Dave. And if Dave's life depended upon it, she had to make Finley believe that she accepted the racing crew's story—that Dave had become an accident looking for a place to happen.

Backing off went against everything she'd grown up believing. If you were thrown, you got back into the saddle. The same thing applied to Dave's driving. If he didn't drive again and soon, he'd come to believe he couldn't. And then Finley would have won, in any case.

Signey gestured at Ken to begin again before *she* lost her nerve, and proceeded to deal a deadly blow to Dave's career.

Then she put on a first-class act, for Kelly's sake, once they arrived in her private hospital room. Jess's act was world-class terrible.

Crouched at the foot of Kelly's bed, he hid himself and put on a ridiculous puppet show with a very pregnant mommy and a smiling daddy doll that the Women's Pavilion provided for siblings.

Silly as it was in Jess's falsetto, he had his sister laughing until tears filled her eyes.

Jess peeked over the bed. Tender mischief lighted his eyes. "How'm I doing so far?"

"Oh, God. Jess. That's awful!" But Kelly smiled through her tears and stretched out her arms to him. He went to her, sat on the bed and folded her into his arms. The puppets lay still on her shoulders.

He cradled his sister in his arms until her tears were spent and she thought she might be able to rest. Then Jess took Signey's hand and led her to the door.

Walking hand in hand down the darkened hallway, they ran into Dave, returning from seeing the kids for dinner at a friend's house.

He looked tired, she thought, feeling her throat still closed by emotion. Desperately tired. His naturally dark complexion had gone sallow. His robin's-egg-blue eyes were as washed out as a pair of old jeans, and his stocky shoulders had a defeated slant. But the set of his jaw let her know how close to the surface his rage simmered.

"You shouldn't have come, Sig. The bastards are sabotaging my cars. They'll stop at nothing. You get in the way, they'll mow you down, too."

Signey nodded. "I was out to the track earlier. The crew was more than willing to let it out that you were at fault. For what it's worth, David, I don't buy it for a minute."

Clearly wound up like an eight-day clock, Dave jerked his head to acknowledge her faith. "Sig, I wouldn't give a flying damn what they think or let out, except that Kelly came this close—" he pinched thumb and forefinger together "—to losing the baby. I'd see Finley in hell if anything happened to either of them."

Later, sitting in the rental car parked in the hospital visitor lot, Jess asked Signey why she hadn't told Dave about Mancouso. Jess had apparently gotten the gist of it from Ken, who'd gone out looking for old buddies to talk with.

"I didn't think he needed any more to deal with. He's already upset that I got involved."

"Ken said it got ugly out there. Said you handled it just fine till Mancouso implied your friendship with Dave makes you unreliable." Reaching across the front seat, he took her hand into his. She squeezed his fingers a little tighter. A little desperately, he thought.

"Mancouso is a creep, a brilliant one, Jess. But I won't let go of this one. If Finley knows anything about me at all, he has to know that. Casting doubt on my objectivity was the only thing Mancouso could do."

Jess pulled out of the parking space. Eyes glued to the road, he downshifted and peeled onto the street. "It could get worse, you know."

Signy turned to watch him as he ripped past the Boulevard Mall and came to a grudging halt at the light on Maryland Parkway and Flamingo. "How?"

"The minute Finley or his lawyer connect you to me, your credibility is shot to hell in a hand basket. Then, not only are you Dave's bosom buddy, you're sleeping with his brother-in-law."

Signey paled. Finley was entirely capable of using her relationship with Jess against her, more than capable of distorting the truth. Las Vegas was about as private a place as a goldfish bowl.

The light turned green. Jess turned right and headed for the Strip. He'd planned to spend the night with her at Dave and Kelly's place. Now that didn't seem like a very smart thing to do.

"Where are you going?"

"To get you a suite at Bally's. I'll go on out and stay at my sister's place."

Signey drew a deep breath, pursed her suddenly trembly lips and swallowed her objections. Jess was obviously not happy about the arrangement, either. She knew in the ways a woman knows such things that the awareness and tension between them would only end in bed. Whether tonight or next week, it would happen.

But Finley would exploit the hell out of it, and Signey resented the power that that conclusion implied.

Much as she regretted Jess's decision, a simple "sorry" felt all wrong. And in any case, he had already pulled into the driveway of Bally's Grand and was escorting her in to take a suite.

She booked herself into a single, feeling very much alone in the very public surroundings, and hoped Finley, Mancouso and their minions were watching.

Jess took her room key from the clerk, and with her bag over his shoulder, walked her to the elevators.

"Another time, babe." His eyes were glued to her lips, but he managed to tear them away and sound casual. *Another time.* As if dinner and a movie were the stakes, when they both knew better.

"Another time," she echoed.

"Soon." Warning or promise? A lazy smile flitted over his features. An onlooker might think it a smile of friendly appreciation for some inane joke.

"Soon, then," she promised, but her voice was breathy. No matter how she tried mirroring his casual way, she swallowed too often and sensed that her own indiscreet expression conveyed far more than her thanks for the lift into town.

"Damn." The way his cords fit now wasn't real discreet, either. Jess touched his fingers to the sensitive skin at Signey's inner wrist and bolted for the door.

HE DROVE OUT pretty much the way he'd driven in. Like a madman. But then, he figured, there was a part of his anatomy so possessed that the only remedy was a cold shower. He turned up the radio, rolled down the windows and shifted into Overdrive, to no avail. Every time he worked the clutch pedal, he knew about it.

He hit Dave and Kelly's place by midnight. The house was dark and lonely, and he didn't mind coloring the air blue with a streak of epithets that lasted twenty minutes. The same time it took his body to ease off.

Far and away too keyed up to sleep, he sat naked in the dark and puffed on one of Dave's cigars. Kelly would be all right, and that eased Jess's mind. Even Dave, having made the decision to back off for awhile, would make it somehow.

But Signey was inescapable. Daring and delicate, her grit vied with vulnerability so deep he couldn't quite figure it. No stranger to risk, he knew the stakes were higher than he'd expected. He was beginning to think in terms of forever. Forever, and not just these few days out of a lifetime.

If the notion scared the hell out of him, well, he couldn't stay away from her, couldn't imagine losing before he'd begun. He was a man sure of his lightning instincts, used to trusting his split-second judgments.

He stripped back the Hands across America quilt Kel had done for her guest bed, stretched out and reached for the phone. He dialed up Information, then Bally's Grand. By the time he'd asked for her room, he felt the pull deep in his sex again.

She answered on the first ring, and Jess thought her voice sounded as strained as his own felt. "It's not just that I want to get laid."

Signey smothered a cry. Her body was like a tinderbox set to light and be lighted. With no chance of either. "I know."

Her response pleased him. Chalk one up to her grit for admitting as much. "What are you doing, babe?"

Nothing . . . sleeping. A half-dozen other fibs suggested themselves and were rejected. How could she lie to the man who'd walked away from taking her to bed, just so that no one could possibly make an issue of her credibility on another man's behalf? "I . . ."

"Anyone watching saw me leave you alone there, Signey. Talk to me. What . . . ? Are you wearing anything?"

His voice was raw, sexy, grating, and wired to every nerve ending in her body. "Flannel . . . a nightgown."

"Flannel?"

"The air conditioning . . . In hotels the air conditioning is . . . is cold and I . . . get cold," she babbled. She'd never had a call like this. Never felt like this.

"But you're not cold, babe. . . . You're not cold. Unbutton it. Undo it for me." Ah, God, but he was paying his own dear price. . . .

Already swollen, aching, her breasts felt better in the cool air than under the sandpaper flannel. Better, until he told her what his tongue would be when it wasn't tied in knots.

Such a sweet-talking tongue. . . .

4

SHE'D DODGED A DISASTER. The next evening Cable Sports ran her story. Filing the same story as every other network had taken the punch out of her conflict with Finley and Mancouso—at least none of her competitors had capitalized on it. But she wrote to Corporate to formally demand copies of the videotapes of both accidents.

Dave would not drive on the Searchlight track again, and for the time being, she could afford to worry only about Corporate's response.

On a personal level, the question of whether to care for Jess was no longer a question at all. Soon, very soon, they would make love. Signey knew it. Jess knew it. Meanwhile the need smoldered and sparked between them. The waiting became yet another game.

Sweet, poignant torment. What would happen afterward, when Jess discovered that she couldn't give him all her heart?

The demands of her rodeo coverage left her little time to reflect. She'd done some exciting segments on the women's barrel racing and the chuck wagon races. A good many of the teams for the chuck wagon races came from Calgary, Canada. And because there were several men to a team, four horses to pull each wagon and another outrider apiece, the sheer numbers of men and horses in the arena made it one of the most dangerous of all events.

Jess had begun campaigning against her fear for him. He wanted her to know how controlled were the risks he took. He'd understood from the beginning that his risks threatened her, and threatened them.

She understood that he had a gift for reading the bulls, for split-second judgment and, like Spanish bullfighters, uncanny hypnotic powers, but he'd cracked or broken most of the bones in his body. He admitted to knowing fifteen men who'd been killed in the rodeo arena, a dozen of them by wild bulls. She didn't find the odds acceptable, and the more he told her, the more she had to ignore her promises to herself.

"CUT!" Ken's voice cut through Signey's woolgathering, too, and brought her back to reality. Today she was at the Chuck Wagon Breakfast, in the middle of her interview with Mayor Bob Regon.

Signey glanced up guiltily, smiled an apology, then put her next question to the man who had been her high school English teacher and speech coach and was now His Honor, the Mayor of Cheyenne.

Backing out of range, Signey signaled for Ken to move in for a closeup. The mayor pitched Cheyenne's unique position as the home of the greatest of all outdoor rodeos, and the crowd that had gathered shook hands with him and greeted Signey like the prodigal child they no doubt thought she was.

After the crowd had thinned, Signey headed toward the tables filled with fresh side of bacon, eggs over medium and pancakes. "C'mon, Mr. Mayor. Let's get in line for some of that breakfast."

She sat for a time with her old friend and mentor on one of a hundred bales of hay scattered around a downtown parking lot, both of them juggling paper plates and cups. Ken parked himself on the pavement at their feet, but Jess didn't join them. He stood a couple of haystacks away, surrounded by fans, and eating a huge pile of pancakes.

Vaguely aware of a spirited argument developing between Ken and Bob—was it horses? Racing?—she sipped at a cup of hot chocolate and focused on her hometown. She remembered catching tadpoles down by Crow Creek and the old library, barnyard dogs, the pungent, earthy smell of the stalls and the warm, welcoming scent of horses. Waking up to the sound of meadowlarks warbling in the prairie grasses. Times when Wyoming had been her whole world.

Though a city by population count, Cheyenne's small-town atmosphere lingered. You could forget you'd ever seen skycrapers that blocked out the sun or big-city smog. Here there was just endless blue sky.

Of course, Signey reflected wryly, the haystacks prickling at the backs of her legs and the down-home smell of frying bacon couldn't be duplicated just anywhere.

"Pretty provincial compared to Atlanta, huh, Signey?" Bob suggested.

"Provincial?" Signey shook her head. "No. 'Provincial' is Easterners who think that we still drive covered wagons into a circle at night. This is . . ." *inexpressible.* "This is . . . Wyoming." She nibbled at a piece of bacon and caught sight of Jess again, entertaining the circle of rodeo aficionados with great gestures.

"Spoken like a true daughter of the West!" Then, as if aware of her distractions, Bob asked, "Watching your girlish figure?"

Before she could answer, Ken interrupted. "No." He angled his head in Jess's direction and cut another pie-sized wedge of flapjacks. "Watching Hawkins."

Signey sent Ken a withering glance, and he countered with a "So-sue-me" expression. Signey laughed. "Both, maybe."

"Well, my dear, if you've caught Hawkins, I'd say you've done rather well for yourself. He could charm the horns off a Brahman bull."

"Don't go jumping to conclusions, Bob. I just met him a few days ago." But she knew whenever Jess glanced her way. Signey crossed her bare legs, planted her elbows upon her knees and sipped hot chocolate. "Okay?"

"Just curious." Bob Regon launched a knowing grin and juggled his plate to shake hands with a passerby. "Turnabout's fair play, young lady. You got your interview and now I want one." Putting on a stern expression that didn't quite conceal his humor, he pointed his plastic fork at her. "What is Hawkins doing here? Word has it he declined the bullfighting contract back in November."

"He changed his mind."

"So much the better. He was the rodeo committee's first choice, anyway." Bob paused long enough to light a cigar, but the action couldn't hide the interest in his wide gray eyes. "I was just thinking maybe you're the reason we got lucky."

Was it the sensation that whoever Jess was talking to at this moment had less than his full attention? Maybe it was the loneliness in her, sparking a contrary need to talk to someone. Or maybe it was just the sun beating down upon her brain.

Signey fixed Ken with a friendly "get-lost" look, and when he complied, she admitted the truth of Bob's suspicions. "You're right, of course. Jess has been traveling the rodeo circuit for several months. He hadn't planned to be here."

"Until you turned up."

"Yeah."

"It's serious between you, then?"

"I . . . it could be, yes. As Jess would put it, he keeps upping the ante."

"Ah." A frown creased the mayor's brow, and he flicked the cigar rather obsessively with his thumb. "Poker can be a very chancy game, my dear."

"I know." Poker—all of Jess's games—were played for high stakes. She'd endured losses before, and her friend knew it. "I'm scared, Bob."

"Of what? Winning or losing?"

Signey laughed. "That may be the problem. I don't know."

The mayor nodded and transferred the cigar to his other hand. "Let's paint ourselves a little scenario here. You've got this stack of chips sitting in front of you. Mind, now, you've worked your whole life for these chips. And you've spent a not inconsiderable amount of time arranging them just so. How'm I doing so far?"

"Okay."

"Good. So you've picked your game, say, five-card stud, and learned all the rules, paid your dues, grown accustomed to the ante. But now you're sittin' with somebody whose game is seven-card. You've got a couple more variables...a couple more choices. There you sit with the makings of a royal flush. Shall we be obvious and say a fistful of hearts?"

"Shall we be blatant and say I'm missing only the king of hearts?"

Shaking his head, the mayor objected. "Not at all. I have no way of knowing whether your Hawkins is a prince among men or a toad. The point, my dear, is this. It's the *queen* of hearts you must draw. *Your* mettle, *your* heart. You're what, thirty-four years old? It's time, don't you think, to take a chance?"

Signey studied the dregs of hot chocolate swirling in the bottom of her cup. "Bob, I just keep remembering something I read once. Hemingway, I think. He hung out with bullfighters in Spain, didn't he? And didn't he write something about not wanting to be friends with them?"

"The man never took his own advice. Why would you?"

"I don't know. What was it?"

The mayor puffed at his cigar. "I believe he said, 'Don't start being friends with bullfighters again... especially not with this one, when you know how good he is and how much you will have to lose if anything happens to him.'"

Don't start being friends with bullfighters... especially not this one. "Why couldn't I remember that, do you suppose?"

The mayor flicked the dead cigar onto the pavement. "To the contrary, my dear. I think you did remember. Not the precise words, perhaps, but the sentiment."

Signey's throat constricted as she felt doubts she could never have admitted. Jess. *Your Hawkins. Your mettle. Your heart.* So much to lose.

"Anyway, my dear, with your style, if the game is worth the candle, you'll find a way. Case closed."

"Easy as pie, huh?"

"Simpler, no doubt. You'll be at the rodeo all afternoon, I hope?"

"Yes. Anything special you'd like us to cover?"

Winking mysteriously, the mayor rose from the haystack. "Don't ask. It's supposed to be a secret."

ONLY THIRTY FEET AWAY, Jess found himself in the clutches of a woman with a liking for cowboys. A determined woman. He was already distracted because when Signey parted company with the mayor and she turned, clearly looking his way, he could see the warm sunlight flush had gone out of her cheeks.

The fact that she was now making her way toward him through the crowd, while he was being treated to a five-hundred-watt come-on smile by this other woman made him real anxious. Would Signey think he'd encouraged the woman? It was broad daylight, smack in the middle of what had to be two hundred people, yet this woman apparently didn't care who knew where her eyes chose to wander.

"I like a man in a button fly," she crooned. "Shows he ain't so anxious to get out of his pants that he won't take the time to pleasure a woman."

Jess felt the heat of embarrassment crawl over him, right to the tips of his ears, like a prairie fire gone wild.

He stood there, feeling like bear bait, deprived of his usual repertoire of refusals. Watching Signey approach, he wondered if she'd heard, and how to get out of this mess?

Signey smiled sweetly, stepped up and threaded her arm possessively through his, then covered the front of his biceps with her other hand.

She glanced up at him, just like he'd fantasized her looking at him, and Jess's heart slammed against his ribs. The minute their eyes met he knew she'd heard and that she was thinking his tongue was in knots again. Then she looked straight at the flirt whose smile was still pure come-on, and laid shameless claim. "Maybe another time."

The woman's smile faded fast, but the crowd broke into laughter, raucous whistles, clapping and cries of "Attagirl!" It was the look in Jess's eyes, however, that made Signey feel warm.

He walked her out of the crowd and kept walking until they reached a remote corner of the parking lot. A high brick planter overflowed with geraniums and daisies. Jess leaned against it, turned and took both Signey's hands into his large, warm fingers, studying her face, as if this were the first time he'd really seen her. He couldn't figure out where the maybe-another-time brush-off fit in with the woman he'd known before. "Wow."

"Don't look so surprised, Hawkins. It's not very flattering."

"Did you think I needed help? That I couldn't get rid of her myself?"

"You were floundering." Signey pulled away from him and turned to touch the geranium petals.

"Floundering? Over some anonymous proposition? You've got to be kidding me." But he was beginning to feel a little warm around the ears again.

"You were embarrassed, Jess. Admit it."

He half turned and hoisted himself onto the brick ledge. "And if I do, will you answer a question for me?"

"Okay, sure. So admit it. You were embarrassed."

"I was." He gestured for Signey to come closer, then pulled her between his thighs until they were eye to eye. "Did you think I'd encouraged her?"

"Why would I think that, Hawkins? I didn't just fall off the cabbage truck."

Jess cleared his throat. She knew he received come-ons like that all the time and that he turned them down just as often. She knew he wasn't going to be fooling around, when there was this thing between them. That if he had a woman, if he wanted a woman, it was her. He could smell her hyacinth scent and wondered if she sensed the heat coming off him. "Guess I wasn't thinking."

"No." Signey swallowed. Sunlight glinted off Jess's hair. Silhouetted against the sun, the shadow he cast was very dark, and his size intimidated her. She didn't know what to do with her hands, except to rest them upon his thighs.

Her hands felt small on his legs. "Did you mean it?"

"Did you think I was joking?"

"No." For that one moment his voice was as raw as a saddle sore.

"I don't sleep with—"

"Just anybody?"

"Hardly anyone," she said. His eyes were so dark it was impossible to call them green anymore. She plucked a daisy trailing over the side of the planter. Peeling petals triggered memories of a child's "Loves me, loves me not," a knee-jerk reaction that seemed ridiculously at odds with her very adult needs.

Eight days ago she'd flown his plane because she couldn't resist him. Five days ago a little voice had insisted that dinner with Hawkins was hardly a lifetime commitment. Now she was on the point of baring her claws because another woman had come on to him. On the point of staking a claim to him. Of making love with him, convincing herself that even those things didn't demand such an impossible promise as "Forever" from her. "Could we . . . could we just walk?"

Sliding down off the ledge, he granted her that much. He crammed his fingers into the back pockets of his Levi's, so he'd have something to with them besides touching her.

After a while, a block or so, Signey asked, "So, what was your question?"

He wanted to know what she'd found to talk about so seriously with the mayor. But he *needed* to know what she was feeling. "What's changed, Signey? Two days ago in Vegas, we put ourselves through hell to seem uninvolved."

Signey shrugged and glanced up at him. "We're in Wyoming now."

The way she said that seemed all wrong to him. As if Wyoming wasn't part of the real world. As if nothing she did here meant anything beyond its boundaries.

He took her hand and led her across the street to a small, brick-paved courtyard with wrought iron benches and sparrows fluttering about. Jess chose the farthest bench under a weeping willow, and they sat down. Releasing her hand, he hunched forward.

"Are *you* indulging in cowboy fantasies, Signey?"

Disbelieving her ears, her eyes darted to his and held. "Jess, I . . ." A shiver passed over her. Why was she forever pitching over emotional cliffs when Hawkins was around? "Why would you think that?"

"Because 'we're in Wyoming now' sounds like something damned temporary. I'm not playing to an eight-second clock here, Signey. And a simple goodbye won't cut it come next Sunday, when the finals are done."

Signey dragged her eyes away from Jess's and stared at her hands. "I wasn't . . . Jess, I didn't mean it that way. I only meant that we're not in the limelight here. In Las Vegas, looking into Dave's crash, I'm a . . . a threat to Finley. Word gets around. No one here knows Finley."

"We won't always be in a place where who we are and who knows him don't matter."

Across the street the mayor announced the reigning Miss Wyoming over a loudspeaker system, and she began to sing the national anthem. The sun poured out a wealth of warmth and light, and the scent of hay and maple syrup hung in the air. But Signey's attention was on Jess's lips. On the small shadow cast by his nose. The scar on his cheek. And on the way his eyes softened as he stared at her. "Always is a very long time, Jess. I think . . . One step at a time, okay?"

"Yeah," he croaked, then smiled. "One right after another."

She got up. Jess rose as well and crammed his fingers into the back pockets of his Levi's.

"Which way to the shopping, woman?"

Signey laughed softly. There was something ineffably feminine, even smugly womanlike about walking around in public with such a man as Hawkins. You could see it in the looks you got from other women and feel it in every accidental touch, knowing no touch of his was accidental. The fact that he wanted to go shopping struck her as funny. "Depends on what you want."

"Costumes. We need costumes for the governor's ball."

Signey took Jess's arm and steered them in the opposite direction. "You need a costume. I already have an Annie Oakley outfit. I even have a pair of six-shooters."

"C'mon, Signey," Jess scoffed. "That's crazy! There'll be a dozen Annie Oakley's. Two dozen—and twice as many six-shooters. What we need here is something different, something...dynamite. What about Pecos Bill? You know Pecos Bill and his girl, Slue-foot Sue?"

Signey nearly choked. "Disney's Pecos Bill! *Heroes of the West* Pecos Bill? That—?"

"Yeah, that Pecos. And you can be Sue. C'mon, Signey, what do you say? It'll be fun."

Signey pretended to bristle. "Pecos Bill was a Texas cowboy, Hawkins."

"So?"

"You're not in Texas. You're in Wyoming."

"What difference does that make? Are you saying a Texas hand isn't as good as a Wyoming?"

"There's no comparison! None!" But her point was all sass, and she couldn't make such a silly statement stick. "Actually, some of my favorite people are Texans. They just have a tendency to exaggerate things to the point of no return."

"Like Pecos Bill, I suppose."

They walked from a store window to inside and out again. "Exactly."

"Look," Jess argued, trying to reason with a woman clearly out of her right mind, "Pecos Bill shot out all the stars of the night."

"Leaving Texas the Lone Star State. How arrogant!"

"He made the Grand Canyon."

"No environmental consciousness at all."

Unrelenting, Jess took her by the shoulders and stared deeply into her eyes. "And he nearly drowned in Slue-foot Sue's whirlpool eyes."

He was teasing her. Signey knew it. But the touch of his hands on her shoulders sent needs skittering through her, and the look in his eyes went from silly to sublime. "Slue-foot Sue had blue eyes, Hawkins."

"And yours are brown," he murmured. "I'll find more . . . other . . . ways to drown, Signey."

Piercing awareness of the possibilities crackled between them. The sun shone brightly. The traffic increased with every passing moment as the Chuck Wagon Breakfast broke up. They stood right in the middle of the sidewalk, while pedestrians streamed around them. Jess trailed the pad of his thumb across her bottom lip, his eyes followed, and Signey lost whatever wits she'd had.

"Play with me, Signey. Cut loose and play with me."

Her heart was knocking beneath her breast, and her gilded, highly paid tongue seemed locked to the pit of her mouth. She wanted nothing, nothing as much as to play with him. She reached up and grabbed the wrist of the hand playing with her lips. And pulled him along, inside the doors of the closest store.

"You have to behave on the streets, Hawkins."

Jess grinned. "Pecos. Just call me Pecos."

They wandered the store until they came across a rack of dresses. Pretty, frilly ones. Jess stopped.

He picked one out, held it up to her and put it back. Then pulled out one he liked better. Signey didn't, but then he found one he liked—one he loved when he held it up to her.

The size was wrong, and there were none left in Signey's size eight. But he happened upon another, a clerk happened by, and Jess proceeded to charm her socks off, point to the one he liked and send her looking for the right size.

Signey seemed to be in a glow, under some crazy, sensual spell. If he'd asked her to try on a sweat suit, she'd have done it. The clerk returned empty-handed, but smiling a promise. She drew Signey toward a dressing room, and Jess was left standing there, hat in hand.

When she came out of the dressing room, Jess was planted on a rawhide, three-legged stool. She held out her arms to give Jess the full effect of the dress he'd picked. It was a Gunne Sax and old-fashioned. Off the shoulder. Ivory and lace, all soft swirls in the most subtle of come-hither styles.

For only the second time in their history, Jess was pretty much speechless.

"Will this do, Pecos?"

She was flirting madly, her eyes dancing, her posture sexy as hell, her sass pure invitation. He ached low down in his body and high up in his heart. He'd ached before, but never like this. He had to smile. When the woman came out to play, the woman came out to play. Somewhere he found his voice. "That's you, Signey."

"The dress?" she asked innocently, whirling slowly to show it off and begging for trouble.

Jess swallowed hard, got up and stood before her. His glance had a way of making her melt, of taking in everything from the soft leather boots to the sparkle in her eyes.

"The dress is fine," he murmured. At that moment he'd have given almost anything to have her alone and out of the damn dress.

"Shall we buy it, then?"

"I'm buying, Signey. It's my fantasy, and I'm buying."

He did. And when they came at last to her car, Jess reached for her.

"Now you've done it," he crowed softly.

"What?"

He wondered how a single word could convey such sass and need and...immodest invitation. "You'll have to pretend to love me, Signey Marie. Grandma Jensen said so. Sue really did love Pecos, so—" he smiled "—you'll have to fake it till you make it, babe."

Her own whimsical smile seemed as permanent as the silly two-step beat of her heart. She had to wonder what Grandma Jensen would have thought of all this.

Especially not this one. The words echoed somewhere deep within her. But it was too late. Signey Marie had already begun faking it.

Nobody did it better.

THE AFTERNOON'S RODEO had seen the serpentine entrance of all the local dignitaries and a few from far away, the Indians, the flags and the national anthem.

Decked out again in his clowning outfit, Jess hunkered down beside Signey as she flipped the pages of storyboard and scanned the notes she'd made for her action coverage this afternoon.

The timed events in Cheyenne included the calf roping and steer wrestling. She had the afternoon mapped out pretty closely, and Jess volunteered to go find someone willing to be interviewed. The man he turned up was Ote James, who came around with his swollen and battered right hand plunged into a half-melted bag of ice. Ken knelt at Signey's side and caught Ote's approach and interview on film.

More like the kid Signey had bandaged up than he was probably aware, Ote didn't seem to know how he was going to get his hand into his glove. That didn't bother him near as much, he told Signey, as wondering how it'd happened.

"In steer wrestling," Signey explained for the benefit of her audience, "two cowboys ride out of a timed-release barrier on either side of a steer. One man hazes in a straight-line dash, while the bulldogger eases over his saddle horn, right onto the horns of the steer. The contest comes in wrestling the animal to the ground in the shortest possible time."

Ote nodded. "Musta been when that durn-blamed steer run me up agin the fence yesterdee."

"And now?" she asked, sensing it had become a test of willpower for Ote.

"I cain't go on injured reserve and collect a paycheck like them ball players do, and I cain't quit, neither."

Signey asked how he could live like that, day to day. His lack of excuses, his determination, his heart were exactly what she was after.

"It's a life what promises nothin'," he answered, "and times don't pay that much. But then agin," he said with a grin, "I ain't got nobody tellin' me what to do."

Signey knew a few hours later that this was one of those days when life delivered up exactly nothing for Ote. He'd missed roping his calf in successive tries and bounced off the steer's hind end for a No Time in the steer wrestling. His Resistol had had come up looking like a tricorne.

In midafternoon the rodeo announcer introduced the governor for the halftime ceremony. Each day honors had been conferred upon men and women who'd brought fame and honor to the state.

The governor called first for a moment's silent prayer for the cowboys who'd died or been killed in the line of work in the past year, then read a list of their names. Afterward he introduced Mayor Bob Regon, who was to announce the special honor to be given today. Caught up in her notes again, Signey wasn't paying much attention.

"We all know rodeo is the greatest sport in the world, but it is still one of the least-publicized and little-known sports competitions in America. Big names in rodeo rarely become household words. No one ever forgets a Hamill or a Spitz or Boitano. Over twenty years ago, Wyoming was fortunate enough to boast such an athlete, a kid whose name was on the lips of everyone. He came from right here in Cheyenne."

Signey's head shot up. Her heart jumped into her throat.

The mayor continued. "He was a skier of the highest ability, a young man whose talent was the hope of the 1968 US Olympic ski team. He died in a tragic accident while on the practice slopes."

Jess watched the color drain from her face. He took her clipboard and pen before they slipped from her grasp.

"While we honor the valiant dead of rodeo this day, we'd like to extend that honor to a man who put Wyoming on the international sports map. His name was Paul Jensen. But we're still more fortunate than we knew, because his sister is home, covering Cheyenne Frontier Days for Cable Sports. Signey Jensen, come up and receive this plaque, which I present by gubernatorial authority!"

5

SIGNEY SAT BACK against the split-rail fence of the arena, afraid to move, afraid not to. Here was the surprise, the secret the mayor had promised her.

The grandstands swelled with a deafening commotion. Thousands of hands clapped, and feet stamped in a rising crescendo of enthusiasm. For long, witless seconds Signey stared at Jess without seeing him, listening to the applause meant for her brother.

"Signey?" Jess shook her gently, but her shoulders tensed. "Signey!"

Her eyes snapped straight to his, followed by a bright, professional on-camera smile.

Jess didn't care for that smile. It was too quick, too practiced. He stood and held out a hand to her. Her fingers were like ice. Something in Jess reacted fiercely and he pulled her to her feet.

She felt as light and fragile as a child, but her eyes bared a woman's mistrusting soul. Hauling her close, he locked her against himself with his arm. Sinking into him, Signey drew a deep breath. Jess kissed her, hard and unrelenting.

He left her no time for kissing him back. "Whatever this is about, Signey, just do it. Handle it." A dare lighted his eyes. "Fake it."

She backed out of his arms and nodded, but the walk across the arena was the longest of her life. The crowd's enthusiasm gathered still more momentum as she accepted the plaque for her long-dead brother. When the mayor called for a speech, she cracked a joke.

"I should have expected this," she muttered into the microphone. "Mr. Regon may be His Honor the Mayor now, but he'll never stop being a speech coach at heart."

Instinct kicked in then. This was her element, and she played to the crowd. Rodeo, she said, was more than the greatest of all sports, it was a reflection of *life*.

She spoke to her hometown, said what it meant to her to be home, here in Wyoming.

Then she spoke of Paul. Her hesitation echoed in the silence and only the muted sounds of livestock and horses could be heard.

"Paul was my big brother. Most of the time I adored him. He lived and died by his own rules. Playing it safe wasn't one of them."

She remembered when Paul had taken her onto ski slopes with the steepest vertical fall line in the country—Jackson Hole, Wyoming. He'd teased her into tears, then out of them. She'd learned dogged determination from him. He'd talked her down mogul-ridden slopes and convinced her she could do anything, just like him, and she had—until he died. She'd never forgiven him that.

She'd learned her lesson well. It wasn't safe or smart to love someone who dared death every day. She covered the microphone with her hand, cleared her throat and looked at Jess. *Especially not this one....*

The broadcaster, the professional in her continued. "*Can't* wasn't a word in Paul's vocabulary. Or *have to*. 'You don't *have* to do anything,' he'd say to me. 'You decide, and you live with it,' But I was only ten or eleven, and I didn't really know what he meant.

"Understanding has been a long time coming, and now, I think, I'm learning what magic it was that came so naturally to him...." But it wasn't courage, heart or mettle that she spoke of.

"Insanity," she quipped, and the crowd laughed again. She smiled and waved the plaque. "I know Paul would have appreciated this tribute. Thank you."

The ground swell of applause began again. Signey jumped down from the podium, and Mayor Regon stepped forward to lead the throng of supporters.

Jess had never seen a woman so clever at hiding her feelings. She hadn't gotten to a position like hers with Cable Sports without the ability to make the most of a public moment, no matter what her feelings. It was those feelings that jarred him to the core.

He couldn't have pinpointed the exact moment when his suspicions had begun to form. Maybe in his plane for the first time, maybe in her mother's kitchen—certainly when he'd seen the brittleness in her doe-brown eyes. He'd told her he was bullfighting, and she'd told him she didn't have it in her to pick up the pieces when he went down.

I've spent all my life searching for what came so naturally to him.... How did the song go? Something about Oz never giving the Tin Man what he already had. Was it heart she'd spent a lifetime searching for and already had?

He sat in the dirt and jerked at the Ace bandage supporting his right knee, wrapping it tighter and tighter as his anger grew. Why couldn't she recognize her own heart? She knew him, knew the need of risk was as much a part of him as the fact that he was left-handed.

She knew because it was what attracted her to her own job, what attracted her to him—what even made her willing to take on Finley in defense of Dave Lindstrom.

But when he looked up and saw her approaching, his anger waned. The sassy, "take that" attitude in her step, the flirting sway of her bottom, the "Look out, boys" smile, all made him wonder for a moment if telling her to fake it hadn't been just a little like siccing the cat onto a canary. The lady had the moves down pat.

"How's that for rising to the occasion?" she demanded.

Her eyes sparkled. A flush flamed in her cheeks. Could she fake either one? He'd never seen her more vital, more alive. Or more sexy. In the middle of the arena, amid thousands of onlookers, he planted his heels in the dirt, gave her a wicked grin, and pulled her onto his lap.

The surprise in her eyes made him smile. "How's that for rising to the occasion, Signey Marie?"

THE SUN was a brilliant orange blur on the western horizon by the time Jess traded in the car he'd rented for a rugged four-wheel-drive, open Jeep. No self-respecting legend would drive anything else, and any other substitute for Pecos Bill's horse Widowmaker would have been a serious compromise. He had to smile at the lengths he was willing to go to set the mood. And those he found himself prepared to go for Signey.

No easy conquest, Signey. But the gumption she'd displayed this afternoon spoke to him, drew him in, made him want her as much as—maybe more than—he wanted to make love to her. Especially if she believed she was faking it. Trying endeared her to him in ways he'd never have guessed. She'd come up spitting and clawing, and that hellcat in her appealed to him most.

He pulled into the circular driveway and bounced his fist off the horn. When Signey didn't appear at the door or call from her window, he pulled himself up and out of the Jeep by the roll bar. He tapped lightly on the unlocked screen door and listened. He heard her talking in broken conversation—a telephone call, maybe. Her voice drew him inside, and he wandered past the sofa they'd so carefully avoided on his first visit, following the sound.

She stood listening, facing a bay-window view of the prairie. Clad in the dress he'd picked, her strawberry-blond hair caught up in a tortoiseshell comb, she beat his imagination all to hell. His gaze lingered on loose tendrils curling softly at the nape of her neck. He could just make out the soft, full curve of her breast.

He'd laughed at his own efforts to insure his fantasy. By his reaction now, Jess knew he'd give it all up, well before any eight-second clock began to tick, to take her to bed. Now.

Signey tried to concentrate on her call. Martha Chin could read the riot act so deftly that Signey needed all her wits.

"Signey, I simply cannot believe this," Martha snapped. "Your letter demanding copies of the videotapes documenting Dave Lindstrom's accidents is simply over the edge. It's insulting...."

Gooseflesh prickled over Signey's arms and neck. She straightened and held the phone receiver away, listening for other sounds. She saw Jess.

He stood, one shoulder propped against the doorjamb in his hips-forward stance. He wore a white Western shirt that molded his arms and lumberjack chest, and a kelly green silk scarf tied like a bandanna at his neck. The contrast against his sun-darkened skin made her already shallow breathing catch in her throat. He was stillness and strength, quiet and power. The hunger in his green eyes mesmerized her.

Some civilized instinct surfaced, enabling her to give Martha a coherent answer. "Martha, I've said it before. If Finley has nothing to hide, there is nothing unreasonable or insulting about asking for copies of those tapes."

Easing the phone away from her ear again, Signey gazed over the prairie and yielded to a self-satisfied smile of feminine pleasure. Jess wanted her. That was all she needed to know.

She turned to him and touched her tongue to her dry lips, with only a small part of her attention on Martha. Jess was across the kitchen in less time than it took her to appreciate his thoroughly masculine intention. He threaded his fingers through loose tendrils of her hair. Her pulse hammered at her throat.

He fused his hand to her nape and kissed her, openmouthed and teasing, as she'd teased. His thumb, callused and hard, stroked at her throat, then sank to her breast. Tremors of response rocked her. Her nipples rose at his touch and tightened unbearably.

Close enough to hear Martha's perfectly modulated voice begging Signey to think twice about what she was doing, Jess touched his tongue to her lips again in a row of tempting, tiny tastes of her, from the corner of her mouth to the delicate arch, then sucked gently at her lower lip. She offered her throat. He touched his lips to her neck. When he backed away, it took more out of him than he'd thought he possessed. He needed her to hang up the damn telephone and come to *him*.

She recognized the sense of loss and turned away from Jess in self-defense. Worrying her lip while heat spread through her, she tried to focus on Martha's advice. She should've been upset, thinking about placating Martha. But Jess was standing there, his weight on one foot, eyes fixed on her. She made some inane, half-sincere comment to Martha about shaping up.

She rang off and trailed her fingers over the phone. Seeing whose need came first became a waiting game between them. Another game, and no matter who won, the payoff would be exquisite.

Jess had known they would come to this, but hadn't meant it to happen now. He'd thought he'd be able to choose the time. Timing meant everything to him, to his life and his risks. Split-second heartbeats. Learning that the choosing was beyond his control stunned him a little. "What was that all about?"

"Finley's attorney filed for an injunction." She smiled. "I'm expressly forbidden to cover anything related to the Finley West racetrack or Dave Lindstrom. We're on to them, and they know it. Dave's accidents are a farce. Forbidding me access clinches it. If I have to resign from Cable Sports to find out what's going on, I will."

That was why Signey Jensen was worth all the trouble he'd gone to. The woman had heart to spare. She just didn't know it.

He took her hands and blew a kiss onto her cheek. His shallow breathing warmed her neck as he rested his forehead against the silky texture of her hair.

That chaste kiss was as intimate as anything she'd ever known.

Jess drew away. "Guess the sofa's not the only hot spot."

Signey gasped for air. "Is any place safe with you, Hawkins?"

He laughed, though he wasn't sure where the humor came from. "Yeah. I'm just private enough to keep from having you on the ballroom floor."

She stroked a loose lock of hair into her comb and pretended a nonchalance she was nowhere close to feeling. The control had gone out of her hands. She wondered if she'd ever had it where Jess was concerned. Drawing her antique shawl over one shoulder, she stepped around him. "Admirable of you. Let's see if you can pull it off."

Signey fell in love with the Jeep. Playing to Jess's fantasy, she asked to drive, and reminded him of Sluefoot Sue's desire to ride Bill's horse Widowmaker. Secretly she knew it amounted to a bid for control. And since she didn't have a wire bustle to bounce her to the moon as Sue had had, it ought to be safe enough.

"What kinda hero would sit still for this?" Jess grumbled in an obnoxious Texas twang.

Signey shot him a smug glance. "This is your fantasy, Hawkins."

He sank into the passenger seat and scowled for effect. "Betcha Sue didn't have such a smart mouth."

"Bet she did." And, Signey thought, she'd bet Sue had needed to prove just as badly that some remnant of her control was left.

But by the time she pulled into the parking lot of the Hitching Post in the west end of town, her hair had blown loose of the comb. She reached into her bag for her cloisonné mirror and handed it to Jess. Their fingers touched, and he took hold of more than the mirror. She tugged her hand from his grasp and ignored the suggestion of intimacy. Letting him hold her mirror was quite enough.

"Put a lid on it, Hawkins, and let me repair the damage."

He held up the mirror for her and knew he could have gone on watching her all night, just like that. Or he could reach out and stroke a finger down her upraised arm and simply keep going, until his fingers touched her breast.

The raw need in his eyes scared her silly. Far from being out of control, she had enormous power over him. The staggering thought bolstered her.

"Jess, if you touch me I won't be able to go in there." Separated by the distance between the Jeep's two seats, their eyes met above the mirror and struggled. She tilted her head this way and that, judging her handiwork. "And if you don't stop looking at me that way, you're gonna look like some calf-eyed teenager."

He laughed out loud, pleased that she'd discovered she could tease rather than worry about their mutually intense attraction. It seemed like one hell of a step forward. He stroked his thumb over the cloisonné back of the mirror. "Is this an antique?"

"Not really. Paul gave it to me."

Jess held it up to her, looking for shadows in her eyes and not finding them.

She plucked daintily at the mirror in his fingers. "Let's go, Pecos."

The crowd was only slightly smaller than at the mayor's reception, but another ballroom had nonetheless been opened. Jess held her hand, and they moved through the spacious rooms.

The crowd was doing more milling around than dancing. A few couples swung in a Texas two-step. Signey quickly became a center of attraction. Clusters of old high school friends and acquaintances gathered round. Shy at first of the celebrity treatment from people who remembered her when she wore ponytails in her hair and braces on her teeth, she gradually warmed to their interest and laughed at the overinflated ideas of her position at Cable Sports.

Jess disappeared for awhile. The governor took to the bandstand, did a number about the great state of Wyoming, and launched the dancing by partnering Miss Frontier Days.

Ken showed up at Signey's side, not a little disgruntled at being preempted. "Old duffer's got his nerve."

"Wrong, bucko," she teased. "He's just got official prerogative on his side." She stood back a little to take in Ken's dandied-up appearance. The suit he wore was definitely turn of the century. "Who're you supposed to be? And where'd you get that suit?"

He sniffed and, not to be left out, led her to the dance floor. "A Pinkerton's detective, of course. And the suit belonged to Karen's great-grandfather, who was."

"Oh! Karen, is it?"

He grinned. "Well, I couldn't call her Miss Frontier all night."

"No. I don't suppose you'd be wearing her ancestor's clothes if it hadn't gone past that already.... Martha called a couple hours ago."

"What'd the Dragon Lady have to say?"

"She wants me to back off Finley's case and quit dragging you into trouble."

"Ah. Finley and his sidekick." Ken grinned. "Are we still employed?"

Signey nodded. "For the time being, but Mancouso slapped Martha with an injunction naming the three of us. You're barred from filming within a fifty-mile radius of Searchlight."

"You ready to quit?" Ken wasn't talking dancing.

She smiled whimsically. "Not for love or money. You?"

As the music ended, Jess showed up with Karen, Ken's rodeo queen date. Ken's shoulders lifted in a "What the hell?" shrug. "Count me in, sweetstuff." Then he looked into Karen's admiring eyes and puffed himself up like a peacock. "I don't scare easy."

Jess took Signey into his arms and eased her onto the dance floor to the strains of "Amarillo by Morning." Somebody cut all the lights save the soft glow from the chandeliers. The crowd hushed, and Jess pressed Signey closer.

"I'd forgotten Martha's call. Were you two planning your strategy or revenge?"

Signey rubbed her forehead against Jess's strong jaw. "Neither. Just a pact, I guess. We're in this to the end, if it comes to that. I'd rather forget it for now."

He clung to her hand as his fingers stroked her cheek. "Yes, ma'am," he murmured. "It's forgotten."

He led her farther onto the crowded dance floor, appreciating the fit of her body to his own, her head in the hollow of his throat, and closed his eyes to fill the rest of his senses with her. He kneaded the small of her back gently. Her subtle scent lulled him, and the vibrations from her throat seeped into him when she hummed along with the music. Hellcat and hyacinth. He'd never been so in thrall.

Signey had felt feminine before this and pretty, but never so much a woman as in Jess's arms, just dancing. One song ended and another began, over and over again. Whether slow or fast, the music accommodated them. Her eyes were closed more often than not, heightening every other sense. Her breasts nestled to his broad chest, her belly to his burgeoning, her thighs against his. Every movement caused her something like pain for the sweet need. He smelled of man, the thudding of his heart was a man's, and the look of him stole the moisture from her lips.

Jess's arm circled her waist. His other hand held hers, close in between them and low, next to her breast, which was bare but for the fabric of the come-hither fantasy dress. His thumb stroked the sweet, rounded side of her breast.

Signey felt hot all over, feverish, yet cold with the shivers of pleasure. He brought her closer still with the arm he held around her waist. There was nothing unwitting or subtle about the way she rubbed against him, nor anything mild-mannered in the response of his body.

"One of us better find some sense, babe," Jess muttered between his teeth.

"Oh? You were counting on me?"

Her look, her smile, the way she shook her head from side to side without ever losing eye contact, all told him just how foolish he was to count on her. There were a dozen reasons why he shouldn't, but he had to kiss her. One kiss, just one. He lowered his mouth to hers, and where he found the sense to make the kiss a brief one, he didn't know. It didn't matter. One was not enough.

He brought his hand to the gentle swell of her hip and backed away until both their bodies felt the loss. Signey stared at Jess, and Jess at Signey. Fortunately or not, the song ended, and the bandleader announced a break. People all around began streaming past them toward refreshments, but both of them were already drunk with needs and longings too long unmet.

Signey smiled again, uncertain what to do or say. She couldn't remember ever feeling quite this fevered pitch of awareness. "Wow."

"Yeah. Wow." Jess risked touching her again to guide her from the dance floor. Maybe he needed that drink, after all.

Signey chose a glass of chardonnay, Jess a double shot of Cuervo Gold tequila. They wended their way through crowded tables, looking for a place to sit. A private, anonymous place, perhaps, a table at which no one would recognize either of them.

Hung up between tables, stuck behind a waitress doling out drinks to a party of six, Signey heard a woman calling out to her.

"Signey, hi! Over here!"

She let go Jess's arm and waved in return, though until she managed to get closer, she didn't recognize the woman.

"Gina? Gina Hampton?" Her raven black hair and mahogany-dark eyes made her look to be in her thirties—at least a decade younger than the midforties Signey knew she was.

"It's Gina Randolph now, though I've lost track of my husband in the crowd. God, how many years has it been?"

Signey laughed. "Too many. I don't want to be reminded." Signey turned to Jess, took his arm again and introduced him. "Gina was Paul's downhill coach."

"Also a champion skier in your own right, if I remember correctly."

"That would have been before Signey's time. A has-been on both accounts." There wasn't a shred of bitterness in her voice, just easy humor. "Actually, my father was Paul's coach—I was there only to help. You were too young, Signey, to make the distinction, I'm sure. Quite an honor the mayor conferred on Paul's memory this afternoon, wasn't it? Why now, do you suppose, after all these years?"

Signey sipped at her wine and shrugged. "The state is becoming more image conscious, I think."

"I suppose," Gina agreed. "It must have been hard for you, though, knowing the way Paul treated you."

"I don't know what you mean, Gina," she said coolly.

"In Jackson Hole. Remember the time our families went skiing there? Surely you—God, you must remember that thing with the mirror...?"

Jess felt a sudden tension drawing in Signey's body
tighter than a rope with a steer at one end and a cutting
horse at the other. Gina's voice had trailed off, as
though she knew she'd said something especially stupid without knowing why. But before he could inter-
vene or Signey answer, the woman's husband
appeared.

Gina cast Signey a sort of confused glance, then introduced her husband around and begged pardon. "I'm
sorry, Signey. I didn't mean to dredge up bad memories. Maybe I'll see you again sometime before you
leave? Jess, it was nice meeting you. Take care, now."

In another moment, Gina Hampton Randolph had
disappeared into the crowd with her husband, and left
Jess with tensions in Signey he knew nothing about.

Somehow he found a way to guide her past the maze
of people and tables. Mercifully a table for two against
the wall came free.

Jess held her chair, then seated himself. "Want to tell
me what that was all about?"

"Not particularly." Signey sipped carelessly at her
wine, expecting the tension to dribble away as the wine
took effect. To the contrary, it seemed somehow to dis-
arm her even more than the careless words of an old
acquaintance. "Not everybody liked Paul. That happens."

Jess reached for Signey's free hand and took her fingers. His thumb stroked back and forth over her
knuckles. "Tell me about the mirror, Signey. What was
she talking about when she asked you if you didn't remember the thing with the mirror?"

She pulled her hand away from him, away from ca-
resses that threatened her. "You don't want to get into

this now, Pecos. The charm of playing out a fantasy is that nothing of reality can intrude to muck it up....'' Jess said nothing, only looked at her with eyes that saw through every facade she had ever set up against him. "Don't ruin the fantasy, Hawkins," she pleaded softly. "It can't last that long."

6

THE BAND PLAYED ON. The ballroom became unbearably warm with the heat of hundreds of bodies, and the party was a smashing success. But if Jess heard the music it was with a powerful sense of uneasiness. Could Signey truly have it in her head that this night, this fantasy was all he wanted from her?

Her silence compelled him to give her another place to start. "Tell me about Paul, then."

From the corner of her eye Signey saw Jess's arm rise to shoulder height. He threw back his head and tossed down his drink, and she wondered if he needed it for staying power. She picked up her own glass and inhaled the wine's fruity aroma. Her eyes so dry that they ached, she focused on light prisms glinting off the chandeliers, on straining tendons in the hands of the guitar player, on the sea of people moving in time to the music.

Toying with her glass, at last she met Jess's eyes. "He was my big brother, Jess. I thought the sun rose and set in him. I thought there could never be anyone else so bold and daring and handsome and wonderful. I thought nothing would ever get in his way." Signey hesitated, seeing Paul, touching his skis, catching the scent of the ski wax he'd chosen. Hearing him. "He used to call me Baby Bird when no one else was around.

Heaven forbid anyone should hear him uttering endearments for his little sister."

Jess shifted in his seat and stared for a moment into his swirling tequila. No one could live up to the inflated expectations of an eleven-year-old; Signey had clearly chosen to remember only the good in her brother. Gina Randolph had changed all that, making her remember the parts that hadn't been so nice, if only for an instant. He had to know why.

"What about the mirror, babe?"

"I told you. Paul gave it to me."

"Why?"

"A birthday present."

"Why, Signey?" Jess jerked his head in the direction Gina Hampton Randolph had disappeared. "What does she know?"

Signey finished her wine too fast, then put down the empty goblet. "This is all just history, Jess. No big deal. Paul gave me the mirror when I turned eleven. It was a birthday present, but he gave it to me because he'd heard somewhere that it was impossible to cry if you're looking into a mirror."

She'd made the mistake of leaving her hand on the table next to her empty goblet. Jess held her fingers again, this time refusing to let her withdraw them. "What made you cry, Signey?"

"Anything," she snapped. "Everything. I was pre-adolescent, Jess. I didn't cry any more than other girls my age, but tears made Paul . . . not crazy, he just—he hated it. I learned to stop crying."

Little girls cry. Women cry. Signey knew that, but she had never cried again. Not at Paul's funeral or Grandma Jensen's, nor at any of the disappointments life had a way of doling out to everyone. She let her eyes find Jess's, then deliberately turned away from his stark, penetrating sympathy.

"Like I said, no big deal." She snagged another wine from a passing tray. The waiter paused, visibly surprised as Signey downed a mouthful.

"You don't need any more wine, babe."

"Don't tell me what I need, Hawkins."

"That will be two-fifty," the waiter put in.

Jess rose, dug into his jeans for his money clip, and although his eyes never left Signey's defiant ones, dumped a five on the tray. His chest had gone tight and dry long moments ago for the child in Signey who'd tried so hard to please, even placate her brother. Even an outsider like Gina Randolph had seen it. If it had been within his power to stomp Paul Jensen into a mud hole and kick it dry, Jess would have done it.

"He bullied you, Signey. Can't you see that?"

"You never bullied Kelly, I suppose?"

Jess grimaced. "There's a difference. A big difference. I'll admit, I'm sure I made Kelly cry sometimes, but I never made her quit crying. Never."

Signey's eyes glistened brightly, and if he hadn't just been told she'd never cried in two decades, Jess would have chalked up the sheen to tears.

"You're missing the point," she answered softly. "I never cried for myself. I cried because he was so good and I thought God would want him back—that he'd die. And then he did."

THEIR PRIVACY was destroyed when old friends happened by, someone asked Signey for a dance, then another and another. Jess wasn't sure he liked her becoming the belated belle of the ball. He decided he didn't like it, but Signey threw herself into the role with a vengeance, dancing, it seemed, with every man in the place.

He kicked out a chair for a footrest from under the table and concluded this must be her way of avoiding dealing with him, with what they both knew needed talking about—why she had it in her head that he wanted just this one night, just this ruined fantasy with her. His expression warned all comers to stay away and he crossed one hand-tooled boot over the other on the vinyl-covered chair seat. He had no intention of joining her in avoiding things, and wanted her to know that right up front.

His nonchalance lasted about two minutes. If it wasn't some hoary old buzzard reaching for Signey, it was something worse. A slick, snot-nosed, corporate type with pheasant feathers sticking out of a jewel-studded silver hatband. Jess snagged a waiter and ordered another double shot of Cuervo. Her dancing partners weren't the issue. Her emotional flight was.

Signey was the most complex woman he'd ever known. She could hold her own in front of a stadium full of people, then seemingly crumble when confronted by the memories of an acquaintance. She could defy a man so powerful in the broadcast industry that she might lose her career, yet believe she hadn't the heart in herself to love and lose again.

He hadn't begun to suspect that in perhaps twenty years she'd never once cried.

He watched a moth flit crazily around the flame of a candle and found himself wishing it'd singe its miserable wings, or that he'd broken that damn mirror when he'd had it in his hands. If he was real honest, he'd admit he wanted to make her cry.

The music grew louder and even more raucous. Jess watched Signey whirl and dip and swing with partner after partner and found himself wishing one, just one of the bastards would give him the slightest excuse to start a brawl. An hour and three double shots of eighty-proof Cuervo later, he'd had it. He might as well have been stone-cold sober.

He kicked the chair he'd used for a footstool back under the table, stretched his legs and strode out of the ballroom, heading for the gift shop. He bought himself an outrageously expensive cigar and peeled off the cellophane wrapper on his way out to the Jeep. Grabbing the roll bar, he swung himself into the driver's seat, then bit off the end of a cigar and lit it.

He slouched, braced his knees against the steering wheel and sat for another hour, dragging slowly on the cigar. He thought once or twice about going back in there and hauling Signey off, but it wasn't his style with a woman. Any woman, much less Signey Jensen.

He blew forty-seven smoke rings before she came out, walking a little unsteadily and hanging on the arm of an admirer. As she approached, Jess heard her giggle and saw the way her escort flirted with her. Something primitive in him flared. He could punch the jerk out for what his eyes were doing to Signey.

He pulled himself up and out of the Jeep and stood there leaning against it, arms folded across his broad chest. He wasn't smiling, and didn't when Signey caught sight of him and waved.

"Jess! There you are! What are you doing out here, anyway? The party's inside."

"I'm not in the mood." He glared at her escort and wasn't misunderstood. The guy dropped her arm fast and walked away.

Teetering a little and suddenly very alone at the corner of a parking lot lit only by an occasional street lamp, Signey felt horribly vulnerable.

Jess waited.

"I've made you angry, haven't I?" She giggled, then realized she should have been horrified and giggled all the more because she wasn't.

"Anger doesn't touch it, Signey."

The alcohol made her careless. "C'mon Jess," she crooned softly. "Don't be mad."

Misreading the passion in his heavy-lidded eyes, she ambled nearer. Much nearer. She placed her elbows upon his crossed arms, toyed with the hair at his throat between shirt and bandanna, and rubbed her forehead back and forth against his jaw.

Wisps of her hair caught on new whiskers, and what had been anger exploded into raging, unapologetic need. Jess unfolded his arms and hauled her closer still. His fingers splayed on her cheek. His thumb guided her jaw upward. Warmth and hyacinth radiated from her body and the heady scent of wine lingered on her lips.

It was the sheen of the skin at her throat that undid him. He kissed her, crushed her lips, tasted and took what was his. He gave her no choice. She'd given him none.

His force was more intoxicating than all the wine she'd drunk. She found herself responding recklessly. She'd felt childish, even petulant in leaving him to dance with anyone and everyone. *So much easier*, she'd thought, to lose herself in a physical frenzy than to face the questions in Jess's eyes.

She wanted to make it up to him, but didn't know how until her body found a way. She returned his kiss, slanting her head and demanding more. It blistered, intensified and excited her. His tongue plunged past her lips and took its toll. She clung to his shoulders and shuddered with hunger and stark needs of her own.

His mouth left her lips and went for her throat. He could feel, almost hear the pounding of her heart in her neck. His hand raked down her back and pulled her hips tightly to him, so she could feel his rigid flesh. So close. He bit at her shoulder, to avenge himself or his anger.

Unsatisfied, he wanted to lay claim to her body in the most elemental way he could. His lips lingered at her shoulder and he sucked until he'd raised a bruise; he held the feminine flare of her hips against him.

He mistrusted her answering urgency. It left him wild for her, unthinking, uncaring, and if it hadn't been for the dregs of his anger, he'd have missed the obvious again. He couldn't make the trade-off she offered.

Now against forever. He wanted more than her body, more than this ill-begotten fantasy. He couldn't forget questions that begged answering, and feelings that craved responses. Tonight, for the first time, he wondered if she were capable of either.

"Signey..." She began moving her hips against him, seducing his flesh, erasing the questions that needed answering from his thoughts. It took everything he had to push her back. Jerking his head toward the Jeep behind him, he released her. "Get in."

"Jess?" She drew her shawl around her shoulders, barely managing even that as she wondered when it had grown so cold.

"Get in, Signey. Now. I'm taking you home." He wondered if the harsh rasp of his voice betrayed his need.

He circled the Jeep with her and almost lifted her into the seat. She watched him through the haze in her brain. A muscle leaped high in his temple. *Still angry.* She heard herself trying to tease his anger away. "Jess, c'mon. I'll make it better, I promise."

He landed in his seat, stomped on the clutch and jammed the Jeep into Reverse even as he started the engine. She leaned forward against the pull of the vehicle's backward motion. Jess just ordered her to put her seat belt on.

His grip on the steering wheel tightened and they were halfway to her parents' home before she tried again. He focused on the ribbon of white lines. When he pulled into the driveway and killed the engine she realized through her giggling, confused thoughts that his anger went deeper than she'd imagined. The awful stillness about him finally sank in.

She gave herself another moment, then reached out to stroke his cheek. "Come in with me, Jess. Stay. I . . . I need you."

He didn't like the sound of that. It smacked of her desperate need to drive old demons away. "Why?"

She shivered, drew back her hand and listened to crickets and the sounds of leaves rustling in the old oak, where her swing used to be. "Don't you get it, Jess? There are no answers. I've been looking for a long time, so I know. There are no answers."

Her voice quavered and she took a breath. He wondered what he would have done if Signey had cried.

He turned, reached out and took her chin into his fingers. "When we make love, babe, I won't need to ask why. I'll know why, and it won't have a damn thing to do with there being answers or not."

SIGNEY WOKE to the gray light of dawn and the warbling of meadowlarks. The sound should have been pleasant, but her head throbbed, suggesting it might explode. She couldn't even remember how she had reached the narrow confines of her old canopied bed.

If only the birds would stop their incessant, cheery song. Just for a while. The muffled, insistent ringing of the telephone broke through the steady throbbing in her head. She groaned, threw back the covers and forced her body up. Bracing herself for a second against the canopy post, she heard a deep baritone voice answering the call. Jess? She let a dizzying sensation pass, then walked slowly out of her room to the top of the steps leading down into the kitchen.

Jess leaned against the counter, arms folded across his bare chest, cradling the phone between his ear and shoulder. Barefoot, the top button of his jeans unfastened, he'd only just come awake himself to answer the phone. Clutching at the button-down fly of his Levi's, he ran the heel of his thumb against morning-swollen flesh.

Oh, God. Her cheeks flamed at the private gesture of need. In spite of her pounding head, an intimate ache settled deep in her body.

He spoke into the phone. "No, Kelly. Signey's still asleep."

Unsmiling, as if sensing her presence, he glanced up at her. A long moment of excruciating awareness arced between them while he looked at her, then answered another of his sister's questions. At last he held out his hand. Signey crept down the stairs and into the circle of his arms while he talked softly to Kelly.

"When did Dave leave?" Listening carelessly, he stroked Signey's back through the light T-shirt she'd worn to bed. She laid her head against his chest, everywhere strewn with hair the color of malt beer. Her hands came to rest upon his back.

"Don't worry about it, Kel. He's got to find out if his backers will still be there if Finley pulls out . . . okay, when Finley pulls out."

Signey tried hard to concentrate on the conversation. It suddenly seemed vital to know where Dave had gone and why. But Jess smelled of soap and leather and warmth. She listened to the steady beat of his heart and felt the vibrations issuing from deep in his throat. She tried again to focus on what he was saying.

"Do you need us to come back to Vegas?" he asked. "Would it help? Signey and— You know damned good and well which *us*, Kel."

Maybe there really is no us, he thought. Maybe there was just Signey alone, just himself, by himself. He closed his eyes, swallowed and rested his cheek upon Signey's head. How much could a man take? Her breasts felt full and warm against his chest, and his erection wasn't going away anytime soon.

"Listen, Kel, if you're doing well enough to hassle me, you'll pull through. Yeah. I love you, too. I'll tell her. Keep in touch, okay?"

He let the receiver fall from his shoulder and replaced it on the cradle. "Sore head?"

Signey nodded gingerly. Her hair caught on unshaven whiskers. "How come you're here, Hawkins?"

He shrugged. "Putting myself through hell. Some people would say it's character building."

He hadn't been able to walk out the door and leave her alone. Instead he'd found some mouthwash to rinse away the lingering taste of stale tobacco and had slept on the forbidden sofa. Releasing her, he turned to fill the coffeepot with cold water. "Any idea where the coffee is?"

"Was I that awful?"

He began to search the cupboards because he couldn't look at her. "Worse."

"Worse?" For the first time she couldn't tell if he was joking. She grabbed a can of coffee out of a cupboard. "Then I really don't know what you're doing here."

He took the can from her, and the incredible stillness overtook him again. "I may be a lot of things, Signey, but a quitter isn't one of them."

"Meaning what?" She slammed the door and regretted it right away, for it reinforced the pounding in her head. "That I am?"

"I didn't say that." Jess eased off the plastic lid and uncovered metal. "Where's the damn can opener?"

"In the damn drawer." She yanked at the utensil drawer, plucked out the can opener and held it up. When he didn't take it from her immediately, she let it clatter onto the pristine countertop and whirled away. "What do you want from me, Jess? An apology? Well, okay. I'm sorry I ruined your Pecos Bill fantasy last night—"

"Don't be an ass, Signey." He clamped down viciously on the can opener. The soft pop of the breaking vacuum echoed in the sudden silence. The aroma of fresh coffee filled the air.

She could have gone on with a list of apologies. Sorry she'd drunk too much, sorry she'd danced too long, sorry, even, that he obviously cared too much. The glint of rising ire in his eyes stopped her.

She sat huddled in a kitchen chair and crossed her arms, clutching at her elbows. Jess measured out three scoops of coffee and plugged the coffeemaker into the wall socket. He turned and leaned against the counter; the coffee began to brew before she spoke again.

"Maybe you want more than I have in me to give, Jess." She'd once told him she didn't have it in her to pick up the pieces if he went down. The truth was, she couldn't begin to wake up with him every morning, look him in the eye and pretend she wasn't afraid for him. "No matter how well I fake it, there's no saying I won't muck it up with you."

"So what? You give up? That's bullshit, Signey, and you damn well know it. Gina Randolph kicked the pedestal out from under your big brother. You'd rather believe there was nothing Paul wasn't good at. Well, lady, there's a lot besides quitting I'm not good at, so maybe you should stop the comparisons now."

"Any poker player worth his salt knows when to fold, Jess. Maybe this is it. Maybe it's all a mistake."

"A mistake." He crossed the distance between them in a single second and jerked her to her feet. He caught her neck in the crook of his elbow, fire blazed in his eyes, then he kissed her.

His hand raked urgently down her body, and she reacted like a torch he'd set aflame with his eyes and his hot, demanding mouth. Needs blazed, raging out of control. His hand found her unbound breast and mercilessly teased. Her nipple tightened, her breast swelled under the relentless fingers.

"Stop it," she begged against his lips.

He let go his lock on her, brought both hands to her sides and stroked. His thumbs reached the undersides of her breasts and continued up, and over, over the tender, aching peaks. "You stop it, babe," he demanded, his voice hoarse.

She had the chance to back away, but didn't. Couldn't. She swallowed convulsively and drew a ragged breath. His lips trailed hot, tiny kisses to her ear. His tongue outlined the delicate lobe as her head dropped to one side.

"Stop it!" she gasped.

His hands sank to her hips and his thumbs pressed at the V where her thighs met her body. "You stop it."

Again he let her go. She ought to have been able to back away, but when she didn't, couldn't for the wretched need in her, his fingers found her panties and breached them, ran along the silk and elastic sides. "Go ahead, Signey," he urged hotly. "You stop it. If this is a mistake, stop it."

But for Signey this was no mistake, there was no stopping it. She forgot where she was, who he was, that of all the men on God's earth, she could not have this one—especially not this one. She forgot everything but the presence of his hand, intimately cupping her, everything but the hot, liquid, curling sensation between her thighs.

Her arms went of their own accord under his, around him. She felt herself grow taut, knowing no one had ever held her like this, and felt her hips roll backward as she strained toward him. She clung to his shoulders for leverage and her eyes met his with still more of the admission. *No mistake.*

He walked her backward. His lips found hers again while his hands cupped her bottom. He maneuvered her past the table, across the kitchen to the back door. He reached for the door handle and turned it, then leaned into her as the door swung open. Suddenly they were out on the porch, in the hot early-morning sun and the lingering chill of the night air.

The cool air touched his hand, damp with her, and a shudder ripped through Jess. With an effort of will that left him stunned with its aching, he pushed her away, left the damp imprint of his shaking hand on her arm. Shaking, because he hadn't known he could want anything as violently as he wanted Signey.

Signey swallowed. "Jess?" Her voice, like his hand, shook.

His eyes closed. His jeans were still half-unfastened and the need of her, the *wanting* had forced his flesh beyond their confines. His eyes opened, green and flaring. "Stop it now, Signey, or I'll take you right here, right now. You got it?"

"I've got it." She took one deliberate step forward and eased her fingers between the strained fabric of the Levi's and cold, hard, metal buttons.

He saw the wild response in her, the wanting that blew needing all to hell. Her fingers wrapped themselves around him, and what was left of his breath hissed out of his lungs.

"Oh, baby. . . ."

She tugged at the last of his buttons, but it wouldn't undo, and she looked up at him. "Help me, Jess. Help me."

He pulled at the open fly until the button gave, stripped off the Levi's and carried her down to the dew-damp grass in one concerted motion.

Their bodies strained together, they couldn't be close enough. Callused, incredibly sensual hands swept upward, taking her T-shirt with them. She lifted her arms and the shirt was gone.

Her breasts swelled in the brilliant mauve light of dawn. She looked down, following the path of his lips as he groaned and bent to cover one pale, rosy nipple with his mouth.

Jess.

Sun-browned fingers closed over the creamy white roundness of her other breast; the sight of his hand and his mouth on her drew a sharp cry from her.

He smiled, knowing from his own needs the extent of hers. Hungry. Lips wet. He pushed her back into the grass and settled between her legs.

"Watch us, Signey. Look at us. See what your body does for me." Touching, tasting, teasing, his mouth drawing at her, her body begging him to fill her.

The cold dew at her back, Jess's heat and the caress of his body drove her. Past all thought, she was beyond feeling anything but the stab of craving deep within her. Hunger. She courted sensations, chasing after them because this was like flying, but better for the mindless climbs and uncontrolled, dizzying downward spirals.

Jess lifted his head and drew in a throbbing, pain-racked breath. Vivid awareness of the sun beating down upon his back and Signey's ardent pulsing at his loins might drive him mad. In another second he would be beyond caring. He had to know. "If this is a mistake, Signey, you'd better stop it now."

Her head still pounded from her excesses. Her body resisted restraints. She wanted him. God, Lord, how she needed him! He'd asked why. To block out the rest of the world? To lose herself in something so awesome, so powerful that she wouldn't have to think or worry whose strength she drew from?

Her eyes opened wide, their pupils mere pinpoints against the glare of the sun. But he gave her no chance, couldn't risk her saying it, stopping what was going on. His fingers found her core, stroked and taunted, and her flesh answered him. She opened herself to his touch and he had his answer. He closed his eyes. Relief? He drew away the silk wisp of her panties, then touched her again in an intimate caress of her delicate, feminine places with his hard flesh.

A prickling at her back, the silken feel of his probing, the soft abrasion of his chest hair on her breast. Sounds and space. She'd never made love at dawn in the grass with endless blue-gray skies above and miles of prairie grasses coming alive for the day. Meadow-larks trilled, her own blood rushed, his heart pounded, multiplying her pleasure a thousand times.

His lips closed again upon her breast. She clutched at the grass and tried to stay still, but her spine stretched and her shoulders drew back as she arched against him, her head lolling to one side. She felt herself tighten and open in quivering spasms. "Lonely," she murmured. *Fill all the lonely places, Jess.* Her hands fled down his sides, urging him nearer.

Something in him exploded. He filled her slowly, moving harder and higher than he'd ever thought possible. To have her, to banish loneliness forever. So fragile, so sweet.

Jess rolled over and took her with him. Suddenly she was in control, lifting and impaling herself, time and again, and at last Jess discovered the ways in which she held her own.

When it was over, they lay together in the grass. The sun beat down upon her skin, upon places never before so intimately exposed to golden rays. She discovered when thought returned that she'd never been so exposed in so many ways. Or so fulfilled. Her loneliness seemed far away.

"I didn't mean to hurt you last night, Jess. I meant to love you."

His fingers trailed down her back, paused and cupped her sun-warmed bottom. "It's forgotten, babe. You were hurting."

Hurting. Like crying, just another way of knowing you were still alive. *Signey Jensen lives.* A solitary tear welled into her eye, then ebbed.

7

MORNINGS they spent together, making love at dawn, selecting and marking tapes for the editors back in Atlanta by nine, lying afternoons in the hot sun.

The dust was thick enough in the rodeo arena to choke a horse. Rivulets of sweat ran between Signey's breasts. Jess would smile knowingly at her discomfort, spirit her off to some dark, empty barn filled with fresh hay, unbutton her blouse and press a cool, wet bandanna to her chest. Following with his mouth, he'd tongue her, touch French kisses to her nipples and bite until fire streaked across her breasts and the pinching ache between her thighs wouldn't go away.

Nights they spent seducing and being seduced. On the lawn. In bed. In the shower. The sleeping bags were great, the porch swing even better. The things Jess had done to her in that porch swing, the way she'd cried out, it was a good thing the house was five country miles from the nearest neighbor.

She had never been happier, never known hours so sweetly filled or moments so rich.

Talking about it seemed chancy, but Jess wasn't about to let her off the hook. In his way, Jess pressured her more than her brother ever had.

Jess's moods paralleled her own. He matched her rhythm, mirrored her hopes. Always upbeat, forever sanguine, he lured her into believing in them.

Her resistance wore thin.

She watched him. He helped her choose the tape segments to send to Atlanta, picking one sequence for its heightened sense of drama, scrapping another to maintain the pace.

She already appreciated the danger in the risks he took. In those hours she began to understand the measure of his skill, the extent of his control. When she ran tapes in slow motion, he could point out to her the very instant he'd known which way the bull would challenge him next, tell her exactly how he would react to counter.

They'd gone to the carnival midway. He'd made love to her ear with his lips in the tunnels. She'd made love to his with hers atop the ferris wheel. She found he coveted caramelized apples but couldn't stand the candied ones. He teased her half the night for the way she consumed raspberry snow cones.

Under the grandstands in the market area he spent three hundred dollars on a kachina doll for her. One with half a watermelon in his lap.

She found an intricate, hand-beaded hatband with a design unlike anything either of them had ever seen and bought it for him.

Driving home from the carnival with their souvenirs—Jess still had the Jeep—Signey stretched within the confines of the seat belt and offered him breakfast in bed.

"I'm talking a serious breakfast here, bud. Waffles and whipped cream and berries and bacon. What do you say?"

"Damn near as close to heaven as you get on earth. What kind of berries?"

"Real berries, Hawkins. The strawberries we bought yesterday."

She knew her defenses were near an all-time low. He watched her beating up her waffle batter. Watched her chop berries, fry bacon, squeeze juice and brew coffee. All because she wouldn't let him help, and he wasn't going to bed without her.

Finally she set a vase of fresh flowers upon the tray with their breakfast, and Jess carried it upstairs.

They sat together, cross-legged and fully clothed on her bed and divvied out the goodies.

She must have been tired. She took one look at him swallowing juice and envisioned him down in the arena and hurt. "How can you not be afraid?"

Jess put down his fork. Pitting himself against wild bulls, day in and day out, somehow he knew exactly what she was talking about. "What makes you think I'm not?"

"You couldn't be and still walk out there...."

"Not true." He shook his head and tossed down his napkin. "The fear is there. But you learn, you adjust, you keep in shape, and you know you're better than you have to be, because someday you'll need every advantage. The day I stop being scared, Signey, is the day I hang it up."

"But Paul—"

"Sweetheart ... Signey, I told you once, you'd have to stop with the comparisons. Some men know they're scared and accept it ... use it. I *use* the fear to keep myself alert to every possibility. I know what's coming at me, and I'm thinking about it all the time. Other guys spend a lot of time denying it. I'm not saying it doesn't work for them, but it's not my style."

It took her all night, right up to the moment she rose from the bed they shared, to get Jess's point.

She wandered to the swing on the front porch, settled back into its cushions and finally understood. It took one hell of a nerve to shoot down mountains at breakneck speed. Her brother Paul had been one of those men who denied that they were ever scared. And it had been Paul who couldn't take her crying; her tears had made him acknowledge the existence of fear.

Jess was different. Special. And she had work to do. She woke him with a touch he couldn't ignore, sleeping or awake. "You owe me an interview, Hawkins."

JESS CAME ACROSS earthy and sincere, as Signey had known he would. She spent the first several moments on the humor end of his job, several more on the courage and hardiness of cowboys in general. Then, after Ken called for a repositioning pause, she grew more personal.

"Tell me about bravery, Jess. What is it? How much must a rodeo clown have?"

Jess let the leather thongs he was braiding into a bull-riding rope slip from his fingers and talked directly to Signey. Ken angled on Jess from behind her.

"You can't measure bravery, Signey. And I think there are different sorts. It takes one kind of courage to stand up for what you believe in and another to stand out here in this arena. For me it's knowing that I'm good enough, that my life is on the line every time a bull comes out, and yet it isn't, because I wouldn't be doing it if I thought I might not come out of it alive." He grinned, suddenly self-conscious. "Whole is something else again."

"It doesn't matter that you come out of it whole?"

"It matters."

"How many times have you been hurt in spite of that?" How many times before this had she wondered and not been able to ask?

Jess shrugged. Reaching down, he picked up the leather thongs again. "A lot, I guess. I've broken about every bone you can name, and I tape up my knees every time I go out there."

"And that doesn't concern you, doesn't eat away at your confidence?"

"If I let it, it might. Someday..."

"Won't someday be too late?" she asked softly. "Can you live only for this moment without thinking about that someday?"

His eyes searched hers. For an interminable time she thought he might not answer. Or that he couldn't. A sense of precious seconds slipping away in silence made her jumpy, but Ken kept the tape rolling. At last Jess angled his head and looked directly into the camera lens.

"This moment is all any of us have, Signey. You know better than most. There aren't any tomorrows guaranteed."

Yes. She knew better than most. "It's an attitude, then."

"Damn straight! A hundred years ago they called it pioneer spirit. It's a lot older than that. The Shoshone had a coming-of-age rite. Their chant went something like this." Jess seemed to retreat into himself. "Plant a thought, harvest an act. Plant an act, harvest a habit. Plant a habit, harvest character. Plant character, harvest a destiny."

Signey felt her focus grow soft and blurry, hearing words Jess didn't say aloud. It was eerie. She was almost inside his head. No. Inside his soul.

Thought. *Trust.*

Act. *Love.*

Habit. *Commitment.*

Character. *Honor.*

Destiny. *Forever.*

Jess touched her hand with the warm leather braid, bringing her back into the moment. Grinning, he cracked, "Kind of deep, but you get the point. Better love today and let tomorrow take care of itself."

Love? Surely he'd meant *live today?* Hadn't he? No, Jess never slipped. She grew uneasy . . . frantic . . . tongue-tied. Had she been thinking straight, she'd have recognized that for the first time since her rookie days, she'd been off balance. *Better live, you mean. . . .*

Slowly his eyes stuck on hers, very slowly he shook his head. *No difference, babe.*

A shiver passed through her. *Reading my thoughts now, Jess? Try this one. This is not the time for your constant double entendres, Hawkins.*

When better? smoky green eyes challenged.

"Gee-awd, this is fascinating!" Ken broke in disgustedly. "I've never seen the like! Will you two hang it up for five minutes and finish this piece? We do have an audience out there. Or should I make myself scarce again?"

Signey felt her cheeks flame in half a dozen shades of crimson, for sure. She waved Ken on, her eyes never leaving Jess. "Yeah, okay. A few minutes." Ken left with a long-suffering sigh. Softly she chided Jess, "We're in the middle of an interview here, you know."

Jess gathered up the length of leather he'd worked and stroked her cheek with it. Warm from his hands, pliant, telling her, *I'll never run out of ways to love you.*

"We're in the middle of our lives, babe. We've spent more time together in the last week and a half than most people do in a couple months. We've made love till I've lost count of the times. Every day I've thought you'd say it tomorrow. Sometimes tomorrow never comes. The hell with tomorrow. I love you, Signey. I want to hear you say it."

The leather was at her lips, her throat, teasing at the very top of her breast. How could she think? The late-afternoon sun glinted off his hair. His eyes, so intensely green now, his pulse bumping at thick veins in his neck. How could she know for sure? *Stop thinking. Once, for once go with what you feel.*

"I love you, Jess."

He smiled without smiling, and she wondered how. He separated the ends of the bull rope, raised it over her head and pulled her closer as the leather strands settled upon her shoulders. She'd found in him magic and power, instinct and charm and tenderness. Now she discovered his capacity for joy.

IF LOVING JESS was a charade, faking it worked. Signey looked up at the clearing sky as a downpour passed and grinned to herself. Leave it to a woman in love to find the joy in ankle-deep mud. Frontier Days wouldn't be the same without at least one gully washer, and this was it.

The arena, dotted with men in long yellow slickers and dripping Stetson hats on horses whose flesh rippled spastically, had become one big mud puddle. When the sun broke through a layer of thunder boomers, the drenched crowd stamped and hollered in a display of undampened enthusiasm.

Ken wasn't amused. "Jerkwater town," he muttered into his mike.

Signey turned down the volume on her headset to tune out his complaint. "Long-suffering soul. It's almost over."

"Can't come soon enough," he returned. "When are they gonna get on with this circus?"

The announcer came on over the PA system then. "Well, folks, that little 'ol rainstorm oughta liven things up a bit! If you'll all bear with us one more minute, we'll take off with another round o' calf ropin'."

Signey grinned at Ken from her side of the arena, nearest the bucking chutes. "Soon enough, sports fan? Isn't this fun?"

Ken gestured heavenward for divine interference. "If there's one thing worse than Signey in trouble, it's Signey in lust."

"Hawkins is wearing off on you, old buddy."

Ken flipped the camera onto his shoulder and scowled into his headset mike. "One more reason to wrap this miserable excuse for an assignment and pack it outa here. Jeez, I'll be glad to get back into my Jag and on the road."

Signey gave up on getting the last word and switched her audiotape to the announcer. Now she had only to fill in the few breaks with random comments. Like a child, she entertained herself with pulling her moccasins from the sucking mud, then hoisted herself onto a fence railing.

Jess and his cohorts were playing again with stick horses, miming quicksand perils and stupidly heroic, failed rescues. A spider monkey riding a Chihuahua sent the crowd into gales of laughter. Then the show went on again.

The roping resulted in a tie for first place. Both cowboys opted for a shared purse rather than another runoff that would put their horses and calves at risk.

For the first time, Signey felt a tremor of concern. Jess could slip as easily as the cutting horses and ropers. She chucked the thought as faintly...well, disloyal. Jess was a survivor and one bent on having fun. An overgrown kid in an oversize mud puddle.

Signey was just looking forward to the final round of the bronc riding when Jess started up some mischief. It sounded like a canned dialogue with the announcer about hearing a lady in distress. She looked around for one of his partners to come sashaying out in a dress. But Jess's eyes lit up and the other clown mimed secret-telling.

Heading for her, miming a pumping heart with his hands leaping out from his chest, Jess shouted to the announcer. "See there! She's stranded up thar on that fence post!"

"Hawkins!" Signey straightened and cast Jess a murderous look. "I'm warning you...."

The announcer repeated Jess's line for the benefit of the audience, then embellished it. "You say she's the most bee-you-tee-ful damsel in *dis*tress you've ever seen?" Jess fell in with the announcer's ad-libbing, crossing his arms over his chest in a broad, soulful gesture. He tripped and ambled and tripped again, imitating a shy, love-struck dunderhead. She hooked her feet behind the rail and threatened eternal damnation.

Jess hollered again. "Help! Did ya hear that? The poor darlin's terrified!"

Terrified wasn't the word for it. Suspicious, maybe.... But before she could react, Jess had lifted her off the fence and confirmed her worst imaginings. Running at full bore to the galloping sound effects of the announcer, Jess took off across the arena. The last thing she heard before her headset fell from her ears was Ken's hysterical chortling. She'd get *him* if it was the last thing—

Jess tripped again, this time bounding forward. He broke their fall with whatever skills and body parts he could, elbows, shoulders. The mud made a fine cushion. But the damage done, she lay in mud up to her ears with Jess on top of her. The only thing left to do was laugh.

Ten thousand rodeo fans hooted, catcalled and thundered their approval, while the announcer heaped haughty shame upon Hawkins. One of his partners tossed him his horn-pierced hat. He kissed her thoroughly behind it.

"Love you, Signey."

He grinned and came up fanning himself, as if her lips had set him afire. Steam billowed out of his ears by some trick she couldn't divine.

When at last Jess helped her up, a circle of Jess's pals closed in around her with a stack of her own fresh clothes, a brand new headset and moccasins, and the Good Skate award; a rodeo clown stepping high, cast in bronze.

The rodeo went on while Signey hurried through a shower and shampoo in a rodeo-committee RV outfitted with such luxuries. Then she threatened Ken with a lifetime of golf tourneys if he didn't wipe that cat-at-the-canary grin off his face.

The bull-riding event was next, with Jess in action. Two heats of contestants were needed to narrow the field and determine the champ. During the first heat, Ken filmed the antics of the local kids hired to taunt and goad the bulls into the chutes. It made for mean-tempered bulls—exactly what the contestants needed for high-scoring rides.

Jess hunkered down just outside chute gate #7 where Sammy Dickerson, a top-ranked young cowboy in line for rookie of the year honors, had more than his share of trouble just getting a seat on the bull he'd drawn.

This ride was for all the money. Her audiotape running, Signey spoke softly into her mike, detailing Sammy's troubles. At last he nodded grimly, the gate flew open, and the bull exploded out of the chute.

Sammy's ride hypnotized the crowd. Thousands of fans held their collective breath. The bull twisted and skidded in the mud, grew enraged, bucked and heaved and lunged. Sammy's right-handed grip slipped, his left arm swung high. He flung his legs to grip the shoulders of the bull. Each second on the eight-second clock encompassed a lifetime of grit.

When the gun fired, signaling the end of the ride, the bull heaved itself an incredible three feet off the ground. Sammy flew off as if in slow motion. He sailed through the air, arms flailing, legs churning. Before he hit the ground, Jess moved in. Signey's heart began bumping in an erratic rhythm.

Jess.

She glanced toward Ken to direct his filming, but he'd already leaped down and run across the slippery arena for a position on the other side.

Talk.... Say anything, just— "The clown Hawkins is whacking the gray, mud-splattered bull across the horns with his hat. The creature is roaring...hunkered down...lowering its head." She raised a pair of binoculars and described the concentration written all over Jess's tight features. She expected him to go for the barrel to put something between himself and the charging bull. He didn't. He turned his back on the animal and started miming a high-stepping panic, running in place.

"The score's an eighty-nine!" roared the announcer. "Dickerson's clinched the title, for certain."

Now the bull began pawing deep cuts into the mud. Jess turned, stuck his thumbs near his ears and waved his fingers, taunting the beast. It snorted in response and stroked deeper still into the mud.

"Hawkins has started running for real now. He's turned his back on the bull.... It's charging! The crowd is going crazy.... The barrel man is behind the bull now, dragging the only thing any of the clowns can put between themselves and the bull...."

Jess turned, crouched and lunged to the side as the bull roared past. Knees bent, his arm shot out. He grabbed a horn, vaulted up with an incredibly powerful motion of his legs and did a handstand on the bull's back, before dropping triumphantly to his feet on the other side.

Signey joined the masses in a wild victory cry as Jess waved the hazers on horses to shoo the bull out of the arena; he began to walk away, accepting the accolades of his fellow clowns.

The bull had other ideas. As if Jess's heart-dotted hot-pink shirt were a magnet, the beast charged again.

Jess read the look of sheer panic on the face of his barrel man and glanced over his shoulder. By instinct he swung low and turned. His shoulder missed a goring by fractions of an inch, but the horns snagged his suspenders and sleeve, and he found himself flung onto the bull's shoulders.

Signey fought down the bile that surged into her throat and forced herself to describe the unfolding scene.

"Hawkins is shoulder to shoulder with the bull, banging and bumping along. His partners are fighting to catch up with the bull.... No way. They'll never catch him." *Oh, God. No.* She couldn't go on ... couldn't watch. But her eyes refused to shut. Her heart hit her throat, her fingers flew to her quaking lips. She was suddenly, inexplicably cold ... so cold. Jess fell to one side and still the bull's horn held his clothes.

For another instant Jess succeeded in kicking his dragging legs away from the stamping hooves. "He's just taken a hoof to the thigh ... another to the ankle." The binoculars brought her within inches of Jess's face, now distorted with pain. Sweat broke out, beading on his upper lip and across his forehead.

"Hawkins is down...." *Swallow. Talk.* "He's face-down in the mud. I can see his shoulders rising, he's breathing hard. The other clowns are closing in. The bull is not interested. He's done, heading for the bull pen." Her fingernails bit into her palms. Her jaw clenched tight against her heart's silent scream. The danger over, her breathing stopped.

"Hawkins is getting up, standing. Shaking his head like it needs clearing. He's yawning hugely." *My God, yawning. . . .* "He's miming, 'Well, that was fun. What's next?'"

Yawning. She would throw up. She knew it. She raked off her new headset, tossed it into the basket of her gear along with the bronze clown and walked away. Just walked, because her heart and mind were out of control, and faking it just didn't do it anymore.

Out of the arena and out of his life.

SILENCE BURIED SIGNEY. She drove home without hearing the car's engine and walked into her parents' house without hearing the birds chirping and warbling over their glutting feast of worms driven from the ground by the rain. Neither did she hear the bees buzzing lazily around the yellow rosebushes nor even the rushing of her blood. Just . . . unutterable silence.

She retrieved her suitcases and methodically began packing. Shirts, jeans, moccasins. She even avoided noticing the gown Jess had bought her to play Slue-foot Sue, though it hung alone in her closet. Her cloisonné mirror. Dry-eyed, she didn't need it, might never need it again. Her grab bag of reporter's tools: mechanical pencils, pencils, pens, press ID, her unused flight ticket to Cheyenne . . .

Should've used that one, should've refused Jess's offer, shouldn't have responded to his challenge. . . .

She never heard Jess drive up, never heard the cane he used clomping on the porch or on the stairs up to her room. But the pain she saw in his eyes matched that in her heart.

"I can't fly outa here, babe. Can't work the damn pedals."

She glanced at his cane, then away, and focused instead on folding her nightshirt. It still had grass stains. "I can't help that, Jess. Get one of your buddies to fly your plane," she replied woodenly.

His voice became hoarse and tight. Angry. And hurt. "Anybody can fly has got their own bird, Signey. I need you to fly me home." *I need a helluva lot more than that,* he thought, *but flying would be a start. Goddamn ankle!*

"Take a bus, fly commercial. I can't, Jess."

"Can't or won't?" Something infinitely dangerous flickered across his pain-etched features.

"Can't and won't. The bottom line is the same, Hawkins. I'm not flying you home." She folded the nightshirt and tucked it with an excess of care into a corner of her suitcase.

"I need you."

"I heard you."

"I want you."

She slammed the suitcase shut. "I can't. I'm not cut out for this, Hawkins."

His cane struck the hardwood floor and bounced. "Goddammit, Signey!" he snarled. "I'm not cut out for one-night stands!"

"We had more."

"You owe me, Signey," he said harshly.

She yanked open the last suitcase and dumped her cosmetics bag and jewelry fold into it. Would he stop at nothing to get his way?

"Owe you? Owe what, Jess? What are we talking about? Flying, or my life?"

His eyes shone again with anger. Or pain that wasn't all physical. "I thought—"

"You thought I could handle it. You thought I could pretend with you and ignore what I am. You thought you could talk me out of being scared. You thought wrong, Jess. Go mold somebody else to your expectations." No.... Don't.... "Go talk to some other woman about trust and love and commitments and honor and forever.... I tried, but I can't."

The phone rang, startling them both. Some powerful instinct in her shrieked, *Don't answer!*

Jess watched her frozen response and limped over to answer it.

Signey watched the color of anger and pain drain from his face.

He said all of two words. "Okay." And "goodbye".

"Somebody sabotaged Dave's Lynx. Cut the brake lines. Are you flying, or am I going to limp out of here alone?"

8

"I'LL FLY YOU HOME."

Someone had sabotaged Dave's own car—his life was in danger again. She had to go. But she knew as well as Jess that his question implied a great deal more than simply asking if she would be there for Dave. The query went to the very heart of their relationship.

Should she take the loving he offered, or turn away?

She needed him to understand the chances weren't so good. "No promises, Jess."

Resting against the four-poster, too weary and caught up in waves of pain licking like a brushfire from his thigh and ankle, Jess closed his eyes. He'd begged her to call him Jess, and about the only time she did was in the same breath with *"No promises."*

But when Signey zipped up her bag, Jess straightened and turned; there was the Gunne Sax dress he'd bought her, still hanging in the closet. He stared at the gown. In that moment he felt as if everything was wrapped up in that costume, everything that had been between them.

Signey swallowed hard at the sight of disappointment competing with the pain in his eyes. Jess hobbled to her closet, pulled the dress off its hanger and limped out of the room.

She saw to the details of closing up the house, while Jess sat at the phone in the kitchen, making calls, his swollen, discolored ankle propped up on the table with a bag of ice draped over it. He called Ken's room at the Hitching Post and got no answer. He called the lounge and asked for Ken Webb to be paged—and got no answer. Finally he left a message at the motel desk and dialed his mother.

Victoria Hawkins listened to his explanations, and he arranged to meet her at McCarran. There he'd help Kelly and Dave put the twins and baby Jason onto a plane back to Reno with Victoria as soon as possible.

Staring at the wall full of her brother's mementos, willing herself not to cry—not to dig into her purse for her little hand mirror—Signey listened to Jess's end of the conversation. He never mentioned his crushed thigh or mangled ankle.

Maybe he didn't want to worry his mother, she thought. Maybe he didn't want to listen to her inevitable maternal scolding. But Signey realized with a shock the real truth was that Hawkins took responsibility for himself. He didn't want or expect anyone to pick up the pieces. Not his mother, not Signey.

A man like that deserved a woman strong enough to stand up to him—to pick up the pieces whether he wanted her to or not, just because she loved him.

In the shiny copper cup of one of Paul's trophies, Signey saw the muted reflection of her fingers flying to cover her trembling lips. God help her, against all reason and hope, she wanted to be strong enough.

She helped him into the Jeep and went back to lock up the house. Any task to save her from having to think or feel or look at that dress crumpled up in Jess's hands.

Jess called Ken one more time from the airport to let him know what had happened, where Signey was going.

Ken didn't take the news too well. "Signey's got to be blaming herself. After that letter demanding copies of Finley's tapes—"

Jess interrupted. "I don't think she's thought about that yet." She was too busy pulling away from him.

"Would it do any good to push for something from the guys I know at Searchlight?"

With the throbbing in his leg and ankle escalating every second, Jess gritted his teeth. "Couldn't hurt. Webb . . . I've gotta get off of my feet."

"Hey, no sweat. Where will you be if I need to get in touch?"

"Try my sister's place in Vegas. Signey might stay at Bally's tonight. After that—my ranch outside Reno." Jess gave Ken his phone number at the ranch house.

Ken hesitated. "Signey will be with you?"

His leg literally shaking with pain, his fist tightened on the lacy come-hither dress, Jess grimaced. "If she's not, I'll know where you can reach her."

He rang off, hobbled out to his plane and hoisted himself into the passenger side doorway as Signey completed the preflight checklist.

She avoided looking at him, his mangled ankle, the cane he'd hobbled up with or the dress he was still carrying around. He was in no mood for her silent treatment, but in no shape to make her face the fact that she was angry with him for getting hurt. That she cared too much to back off now.

Signey sat there for a moment, lost in thought, almost as though she'd forgotten what to do next. "Might help if you turned on the engine, babe."

Quick and ferocious, her sideways glance took in everything she'd been avoiding.

"This is November-Tango-One-Niner-Four-Niner. Am I clear for takeoff?"

"Affirmative, Niner-Four-Niner. There's a beauty of a sunset!"

Signey lifted off at 1940 hours into the sunset, minus the happily ever after. Jess was in a great deal of pain, if his gray-cast flesh, drawn tightly over his cheeks, was any indication. He ought to be in the hospital under medication. She hadn't expected him to be so stoically silent.

She hadn't expected him to drag her dress everywhere with him, either. But she knew why he was doing it. She knew exactly why. Every time she looked at that dress she had to remember, had to think how much she'd already promised him.

She found herself incapable of enjoying the pilot's seat. The horror of Jess's close call had shoved a wedge between them. And oh, God, was he hurting!

Her pretense, faking it for Jess, seemed all the more shallow now. At first he'd urged her to fake loving him until she really could. She did love him; she knew that. The real pretense, the make-believe she could handle her fears for Jess in the arena—that was another story altogether.

She saw his jaw tighten. His grip on the cane harden. Eyes closed, he seemed to be trying to rest, but sleep probably had no chance to overcome the throbbing pain. Tenderness welled in her.

Somehow she had to make him understand. A man could be scared on his own account. He might even take his woman's fears for proof of her love. But Signey knew that if she hung around Jess long enough, sooner or later her fears would poison their relationship. He refused to understand.

She just had no faith that her terror wouldn't finally inspire an unreasoning anger in him. Or loom so large that he'd forget why he'd ever loved her.

Bitterness clogged her throat. She wanted to be strong enough for him. But she wasn't.

"Are you going to be okay?" Jess asked quietly.

Startled out of her reverie, Signey looked out the cabin window at the craggy tops of mountain ranges, peaks that reminded her of insurmountable odds. That reminded her of poker. Upping the ante and living with it, win or lose, and Hemingway's caution. *Especially not this one.* "Yeah."

"You had a knee-jerk reaction, babe. Plain and simple." Why was he trying to talk her out of her feelings?

"Knee-jerk?"

"Reflex. See Hawkins in mortal danger. Panic. Knee-jerk. You're better than that, Signey. You just have to realize you are."

"I'm not as resilient as you think, Jess."

Shifting in his seat, he put unexpected pressure upon his ankle and swore. "Dammit, Signey, I'm not up to arguing with you."

"Then don't."

His breath exploding out of him, he sank back in his seat and closed his eyes again. She loosened her death grip on the yoke and concentrated on flying.

She wasn't proud of threatening to leave, or of tell-ing him to get someone else to fly his plane home for him, but her reaction had been honest. He'd once said the odds of being maimed or killed in the arena were less than the chances of being run over on a street corner— or of crashing the Bonanza into the nearest mountain range.

The odds didn't make a damn bit of difference when it happened.

Her heart twisted in shame when Jess slipped her come-hither dress into the side pocket of her suitcase.

SHE TOUCHED DOWN at McCarran International within moments of the commercial flight Victoria Hawkins had taken from Reno. A honeyed blonde, Victoria wore tweedy colours accented with outrageous oranges that clashed with the airport's vibrant purple hues. One for Victoria, zero for the garish interior design. So this was where Jess had gotten his one-up tendencies.

Kelly and Dave arrived by courtesy car from Bally's Grand Hotel. Their somber mood hadn't infected the three white-blond kids, Cammie and Danny, the five-year-old twins, and one-year-old Jason.

Chorusing in unison, "Aunt Sig! Uncle Jess! Gramma Vic!" the kids clearly couldn't quite believe the good luck of having all their favorites in one place at the same time.

"Aunt *Sig?*" Victoria grimaced. Glaring at Jess's cane and bootless foot, it was obvious she'd latched on to the first topic of conversation to avoid a scathing, the-only-difference-between-men-and-boys remark. "Kelly, are your children constitutionally incapable of pronounc-ing a name longer than a single syllable?"

Signey instantly wondered why it was so much easier for women to criticize their daughters rather than their sons. On the other hand, she found herself in total sympathy with Victoria on both accounts—Jess's injuries and the title "Aunt Sig," which somehow smacked of a matchmaking conspiracy.

Squelching the urge to make that accusation, she feigned ignorance instead. "No accounting for the 'aunt' part. It's new to me. 'Sig' is Dave's fault."

Signey could almost hear Jess coming out with an unsuitably irreverent comment about the conjugal suitability of 'Aunt' Sig. She shot him a warning look and returned Victoria's impulsive hug. Later she'd remember how quickly Jess had gotten past the tension between them, and the sharp disappointment of having had to beg her to fly him home.

"Well, welcome to the family anyway, my dear. I'm so pleased to meet you. Hadn't we better see to my return flight?"

It took every minute of the hour that followed to get the three kids and Victoria fed and safely onto the flight home. Afterward Jess and Kelly settled themselves on one side of the airport lounge booth, Dave and Signey on the other.

Having decided the near-empty lounge was as good a place as any to talk, Signey listened to his story, beginning to end. Months ago he'd begun to suspect that the cars he drove were not being maintained properly, he told her.

When at last he ended, Signey asked, "Dave, is there anyone, anyone at all you can think of at Finley West who felt as uncertain about the cars as you?"

"Half the crew!" Dave shrugged doubtfully. "Everyone knew there wasn't quite the same quality there, Sig. But John Cragen—"

"Cragen from your pit crew?"

"Yeah. The guy hasn't looked me in the eye in weeks."

Signey wrote Cragen's name on a napkin to check into later. "Do you think Cragen might be involved in sabotage?"

"I don't know, Sig. I'm just sick of the whole damn thing. And then they have the goddamn nerve to come after my own car."

Signey paled, wondering for the first time why they'd have come after Dave's personal property. "Dave, it was probably the letter I sent—"

Dave cut her off harshly. "That's ridiculous, Sig. They were no more threatened by your letter than nothing."

"Then why, Dave?" Jess asked. "Why else would these jerks sabotage your car?"

Dave shifted uneasily in the booth. Signey and Jess exchanged glances.

Dronelike, Dave filled in the missing parts. "I spoke to some other investors, some other guys who might be willing to sponsor me. Jimmy Carver set me up with a few of these guys last Saturday. After that, I drove out to the track, bounced my briefcase off my manager's desk, told him I knew exactly what was going on, dropped some names and—"

"Threatened him," Signey concluded. "Oh, Dave..." She didn't have to wonder, knowing Finley's attorney Mancouso, exactly how Dave's threats could be used against him.

Nor did she need to wonder how anything she could do for Dave could be turned against them. She could hear Mancouso repeating a list of charges against her, headed by conflict of interest.

"So . . . what do we do now?" Kelly questioned.

"I'm assuming you've been to the police?"

Dave nodded. "No way to keep them out of it. I couldn't keep the Lynx from slamming into the guardrail. The cops get real curious when they find a brake line tampered with."

"Then we'll take the whole mess public," Signey said. "Everybody does it these days. The only way to bring the issues out into the open is to force a response. Finley can't afford not to answer."

Straightening to ease the pain in his leg, Jess unlocked his teeth enough to object to her strategy. "Signey, you can't go blaming the sabotage to Dave's car on Finley with no proof!"

"No," she replied, "but we can suggest a conspiracy by Finley to defraud the investors in his backers' consortium. And Dave isn't the only one who saw those cars go begging for attention."

Hurting, tired, impatient, Jess wanted to know why Dave didn't just stand up and make his own statement.

"That almost always comes off unsympathetic, Jess—like whining," Signey told him. But when she turned to look at him, he shook his head. "What are you thinking, Jess? That I can't do this?"

Arm slung over the back of the booth, Jess rolled his eyes. "You're just contrary enough to try, no matter what I say. You're cruising for a black eye, which Mancouso will be more than happy to deliver."

"And you're in no position to talk to me about getting hurt!"

"Oh, fine!" Jess exploded. He had no painkillers, but he'd thought the liquor might have dented the pain roaring through him. No such luck. "If I were a goddamn carpenter and I came home with a smashed thumb, would you go out and throw yourself in front of the nearest train?"

"I'm not doing this to get even with you."

"And all I'm saying is that if you're smart you'll back off with no bad feelings and let us find another hired gun."

"Oh, stow the judgments from on high, Jess," Kelly snapped. "Signey knows we'll understand if she can't do it."

He matched Kelly glare for glare. "You know she'll do it."

"I don't know that at all. But don't you think you might let her decide?"

"No. She'll do this and lose everything she's spent a lifetime building. If she wants to be here, fine. In the background. You're asking too much. There are some very pricey, nasty lawyers out there."

Signey watched Dave tune out the sibling battle between Kelly and Jess and order his fourth draft beer. His head was cut, bruised and stitched just above his right eyebrow. She guessed his psyche was bruised far, far worse. Dave didn't drink. Period. Both men were battered messes, and that goaded her into making a decision.

She listened to Jess arguing against involving her. He made a good case, except that if Finley had come to this, to ensuring that Dave wasn't around to talk, even if they had to sabotage his personal property, then she could no longer work for him, anyway.

This had nothing to do with whether or not she'd ever work in the industry again, and nothing to do with whether Jess thought she could handle the consequences.

Contrary or not, she'd handle Dave's public charges and deal with the aftermath, as well.

"You might as well quit arguing, Jess, Kelly. I'll call a press conference for morning. I'm going to take this public and see it through."

THEY LEFT for Bally's Grand, and once there Signey flashed press credentials and dropped names until she got to see the management. She didn't hesitate to pull every string her Cable Sports connections offered.

"I want a ballroom suitable for a press conference. I'd like a setup for a bank of microphones, including a podium and access for the press. I'd like to get word out on the wires tonight that a press conference will be held on behalf of Dave Lindstrom, detailing the recent occurrences on his racetrack." Signey tossed out her demands, and the night management snapped more or less to attention.

Jess watched her wheeling and dealing until she got what she wanted, the room, the time and promises of coffee and rolls. Signey was clearly on her turf, and all Jess could do was put on a show of resigned anger at her nonchalance. Kelly offered to go upstairs with him, and he hobbled off with his sister toward the bank of elevators. Only then did he let a crooked, calculating grin overcome the grimace on his face.

The light dawned for Kelly. "You utter creep!" she accused him. "You've been playing devil's advocate all night!"

"Stow the judgments from on high, Kel," he threw back at her. "I've got my reasons."

"You're despicable."

"I know." He thought for a second that he might just collapse with the pain.

"Oh, Jess! How can I holler at you when you make faces like that?"

Gritting his teeth, he shot back, "You can't."

"Mind telling me what's going on in that twisted mind of yours?"

"Look, Kel, Signey can pull this off. If we need to bring in some big guns, we will. But once she finds out she really can handle Finley, she'll realize she can handle anything. Hell, it's too damn complicated to explain." *Maybe too complicated, period.*

"You had to be there, I guess," Kelly teased gently, trying to ease laughter into his eyes to counter the pain etched all over his face. The scar on his cheek had gone white.

"Yeah. You had to be there." He kissed her good-night and hobbled to the suite next door. Blackness, welcome, stark blackness closed over him as he fell onto the bed.

KEN CALLED at around 2:00 a.m.

Signey snatched the receiver out of the cradle on the first ring and relaxed in the wing chair in Jess's suite. The last thing she wanted was to have his already fitful sleep disturbed. Half comatose, half delirious, he hadn't awakened when she'd come in, when she'd ordered up ice packs, or when she'd stripped off his jeans and tended his thigh and ankle.

She'd been around athletic trainers and done enough herself under their instruction for her stories to be able to recognize the extent of the damage Jess had suffered. The clotting possibilities of the bruise on his thigh, for instance, would concern a physician. The part of her that was the woman in love screamed bloody murder. The bruise was angry looking and hot to the touch, purple and swollen and black.

She'd spent the hours working and reworking her statement for the ten o'clock press conference and changing the compresses, so Ken's phone call came as a relief.

"Cheyenne in my rearview mirror. How sweet it was! I drove all day. How's Hawkins?"

"Sleeping. Hard to get along with. Fed up. That about covers the territory."

"No doubt. What about Dave?"

"I've been working on a press release I'm issuing in the morning on his behalf."

"I take it you're about to commit professional hara-kiri?"

Signey choked on a swallow of cold cocoa. "Jess would appreciate that line. As a matter of fact, yes. I have to resign, Ken. Finley was always borderline, but I told myself I was working for Martha, that Finley... I can't do that anymore, Ken. I just can't."

"Are you worried about Martha understanding that, or..."

"No. Martha will know why I had to do this." But while she was having no second thoughts about her decision, she couldn't ignore the regrets for leaving behind other people, colleagues she'd grown to care for. Regrets she couldn't afford to indulge in at the moment. "The situation *is* very bad, Ken. Have you talked to any of your old cronies?"

"Yeah. Everybody's spooked. Won't touch the subject of Dave Lindstrom with a ten-foot pole. One name came up, though. Do you know a John Cragen?"

Signey straightened and set down her cocoa. Cragen was the one name Dave had mentioned in the lounge at the airport. All she needed was one man willing to back Dave's hunches. Just one. "Why?"

"No one knows where the guy is, sweetstuff. Common wisdom has it, if he knew something, he'd have a real good excuse for getting himself lost. Mancouso seems not to be the forgiving sort."

"Great. What do we do now?"

"Make your statement and let the chips fall, I guess. Use his name in your press conference."

She'd already doodled Cragen's name on the margin of her notes. "Ken, I really hope your involvement doesn't get you fired at Cable Sports...."

"Not to worry, you hear? Just ... take care of yourself, take care of Hawkins, and let me hear from you someday soon. Okay?"

Take care of Hawkins. Even now, listening to Ken, Jess's uneasy breathing caught at her heart.

Distracted by the sound, Signey ended the quiet conversation with Ken. "I'll do that, Ken. And ... thanks. I owe you."

"Nothing. You owe me nothing, sweetstuff. Take care now, you hear?"

She returned the receiver to the phone cradle, then switched off the lamp beside her, as well. Only a prism of light seeped through the sitting-room doorway.

For a moment she sat massaging her eyes, then got up and pulled back the curtains. Dependably, Vegas was alive with neon glitz and all the veneer of glamour she could stomach.

She found herself longing for Jess's ranch, even though she had already made up her mind not to go with them when Jess took Kelly and Dave back to Reno.

His breathing suddenly grew more erratic, and his restless movements sent her flying to his side. She switched on the lamp, eased his hair from his brow, crooned softly to him. "What is it, Jess? Your thigh, your ankle?"

He croaked something about his whole damn body, then threw back the covers and began to sit up.

"Jess, stop it and lie down!"

"So wet."

Easing her arm beneath his head, Signey urged him down. "I know. I'll take care of it. Please, Jess, just lie down."

He gave up then and sank back, watching her ministrations.

She went to the other bed and stripped linens to pad the soaked area, then discovered just how wet and cold he was. Right up to and including his Jockey shorts.

The look on her face was priceless, even in his half stupor, and he laughed. If he hadn't hurt so badly, maybe he wouldn't have laughed so hard, but it was a damn sight easier than crying.

"Where's another pair?"

"In my duffel bag." She turned to find it, but the sound of his voice croaking softly at her made her turn back. "The duffel's still in the plane."

"Hawkins, you can't leave those on. They'll just get the new sheets damp."

"I know." He angled himself up and onto his elbows.

"You'll have to get out of them." She busied herself with folding the extra sheets to a manageable size.

"I know."

"Then for God's sake, get out of them!"

"I can't." He fell back onto his pillows. His head hurt—probably a minor concussion—his back had been wrenched and ached from lying in the same position, and if he had to get his own shorts off, his butt would freeze before it happened. He wasn't laughing anymore. "I can't. You'll have to do it."

Clutching the sheet to her breast, she said, "Oh . . . damn."

"Signey."

Said like that, her name was a gentle scolding. *You've seen me*, it said, *all of me. Touched, stroked, taken me with your sweet lips.*

She swallowed. What could he do with his nudity and her hands, after all, and in his condition? Her lip trembled stupidly as she discovered she had no choice but to pick up the pieces.

She tucked dry sheets beneath him, and he knew what she was feeling. She was incensed with him for getting hurt, for lying there wounded, and for making her see that picking up the pieces was just something a woman sometimes had to do, and that she was that woman. Her angry brown eyes looked a lot like her passion-filled eyes when he made love to her.

She bent toward him and her fingers curled around the elastic band at his lean, muscled hips; her eyes were glued to the bulge she uncovered and she swallowed again. How contrary, to think how masculine, how beautiful, how male he was, when he lay there helpless and needing her to tend him in . . . other ways.

"You promised me, Hawkins."

"Promised you what, babe?" His voice was low and hoarse and full of an emotion he hadn't experienced before and couldn't figure.

"Bullfighting is—most of the time, you said—just boring." She eased the Jockey shorts over his thighs, then his knees and finally his swollen ankle. She forced her gaze to follow her fingers, but that made no difference. How contrary to notice stiffly curling, malt-colored hair. The size of him. The need thickening him. Her voice was reduced to a whisper. "Safer than crossing the street, you said."

A man could endure a woman's hands, but not those heated eyes and not that voice. Not without his body reacting. In one wild, sweet rush his naked body hardened. "Things . . . happen."

"Jess," she whispered.

Without thinking she knelt on the floor beside him and took his whiskered face between her hands. He made no move toward her, to hold her or push her away. Naked as the day he was born and rigid, he needed her to love him when he was all beat to hell like this as much as, no, *more* than when he was healthy. He closed his eyes, enduring . . . savoring yet another ache.

"Jess..." Signey's voice trailed off because she didn't know what to say, how to explain the fact that she was still here, picking up his pieces. Still here, about to kiss him, about to close her hand around him. "Jess..."

Her mouth came close, lowered, trembled. Her lips brushed his. She repeated the caress against his jaw. A third time to the raggedly pulsing point near his throat. Again and again, lower each time, lingering, pressing her lips harder until they grazed his nipples and her teeth echoed the gesture. The shock of pleasure and sensation shot through Jess and tore a groan from deep in his throat.

His wound drew her attention, the swelling, the heat, and she touched her lips to his hurt as though her kiss might heal him. She wanted to heal him, wanted to be the one to make him whole again, wanted it to be her caress, no one else's. And she knew how contrary to her own survival that was, too. This time he'd walked away. Next time he might not.

Especially not this one. Her hand closed around him. Warm and rigid, softer than satin and thicker than her hand could grasp, it was good, very good, but not nearly enough. Her eyes flew to his, questioning. *How can I do this?*

She knew, and they moved in perfect concert. She kicked off her sandals, he lifted her skirt. She knelt next to him on his bed, he offered her a steadying hand. Carefully, carefully, she straddled his body, and his fingers both stroked her and held aside her panties. Signey took him into herself, and he felt better than he had in hours and hours, just sheathed, at home.

Neither moved. He reached for the butttons of her blouse, and for every one that came loose, he flexed his hips and pushed himself higher into her. Breathing ragged, fingers clumsy, his tolerance blown to hell and back, yet when he was done and had pushed aside the soft fabric, there still remained her bra.

"Undo it for me, babe."

She shrugged out of her blouse, unhooked her bra, and he drew it down, slowly, achingly slowly down, then threw it aside. Signey began a gently rocking, flexing motion of her hips, and Jess echoed the rhythm with his thumbs, flicking them back and forth over her tight peaks until her nipples were rigid and straining. She moaned and her hips gathered momentum, rocking wildly. His fingers plucked at her nipples, urging her on, on, on. She rode her wounded warrior for all she was worth and more.

When it was over, when she lay in the tangle of her skirt, the sheets and his undamaged leg, the pain that had never been very far away reclaimed him, redoubled. He tried to hide it from her, but she saw the agony behind his smile, in the harsh lines on his brow and the tightening of his lips over clenched teeth.

She promised herself that this was the last time she would be there to pick up his pieces. Or love them, either. But even as she swore, *Especially not this one*, she had no idea how she'd make good that promise.

9

SEVEN HOURS LATER Signey faced the glaring lights, a bank of microphones and a swamped conference room with her carefully conceived statement on Dave Lindstrom's behalf. The gauntlet was about to be thrown at Finley's feet.

"Good morning. I'm Signey Jensen and I'd like to state for the record that the comments I'm about to make are on behalf of David Lindstrom, his family and myself and have nothing to do with my position with Cable Sports—to which I now tender my resignation. That said, I'd like to make a full statement, without interruption, and then I'll field any questions you may have."

She paused discreetly to wipe her sweating palms on a handkerchief and acknowledge with a nod Jess's gesture of encouragement.

"These are the facts as Dave Lindstrom knows them." She described the crashes of two experimental cars and the accounting reports he'd seen, each budgeting a million dollars to research and development, each account detailing the expenditures in excess of a million dollars.

"Dave is not an accountant, nor is he all that familiar with R and D accounting principles. But he knows the quality of the cars he drove and he knows how many times the velocity stacks were replaced, the manifolds adjusted, or the suspension systems beefed up. We would like to know what has become of a Mr. John Cragen, a member of Dave's pit crew for the last several years. Mr. Cragen seems to have disappeared at this crucial juncture. And he, as well as Dave, knew that the two cars didn't come close to a million dollars' each worth of quality.

"Dave complained," Signey went on, intending with a bedrock honesty about Dave's temper to appear scrupulously unbiased and fair. "He ranted and raved and yes, slammed his crash helmet into the retaining wall on his own practice track. A few days ago, deep in his frustration over events seemingly beyond his control, Dave threatened Finley West management. Even before that, however, Walter Finley, director of the consortium of Dave's backers, pulled all support, and attempted to poison the minds of the investors. Dave's personal car has since been sabotaged, as well."

She concluded with an unforgiving indictment of Finley, of a system that condemned the driver and condoned the Machiavellian manipulations of one man.

"Dave has spoken to financial analysts who believe Walter D. Finley may very well be mired in financial problems. There are investors who suspect that Finley has misappropriated investor funds, diverting them to bail himself out. Dave will turn over the names of all these people to the authorities and then begin seeking new backers."

She answered questions until there were no more. Then she saw the independent stringer, a Nevada native Cable Sports had used in the past. Philip Mancouso, Finley's lawyer, stood at the stringer's side, feeding him questions.

"Ms. Jensen, could you tell when you decided to resign your position at Cable Sports?"

"I made the decision last night."

"Are you saying you suspected Walt Finley since the first of Lindstrom's crashes—all this time—and yet you continued to work for Cable Sports?"

Signey hesitated. Jess had asked her the same question ten days ago. "I like to believe," she said, addressing the stringer, "that my actions are not based on snap judgments. It is widely known that my philosophy and Mr. Finley's have been widely divergent for many years, and that for the good of the network we . . . agreed to disagree. I am simply no longer willing merely to disagree."

"You credit yourself with caution, and yet you're willing to stand here implicating a pillar of the sports community in the sabotage of Lindstrom's car!"

Signey shook her head. Her heart was thudding wildly, but she knew her voice, her gilded, highly paid tongue gave no hint of her stress. "I said only that Dave's car had been sabotaged. You drew your own conclusion."

A DOZEN HOURS LATER, curled up in an easy chair at Dave and Kelly's ranch house outside Las Vegas, Signey watched a videotape of herself on the evening "Cable Sports News Hour."

Cable Sports announced her resignation and ran the entire press conference, devoting an unprecedented amount of time to a single issue. They used the time outside Martha Chin's area of influence, and willingly, Signey knew. They interviewed other drivers and other pit crews with the intent to make Dave appear more than slightly paranoid, then ended with calling her "wildly irresponsible in abandoning the sacred trust of journalistic impartiality and integrity."

She hadn't expected a garden party, but the accusations stung, and she had to wonder if some smoking-guns attorney wouldn't have done better, after all.

Kelly, heavily pregnant, her swollen feet up on the couch, used the Remote to switch off the VCR and television. "Come on, Signey. Give it up."

Signey could hear Dave and Jess in the next room, roaring at each other over the billiard table—something about using a cane for a pool cue—but the humor of their jubilant mood escaped her. "I wish it had gone better. Life isn't very fair, is it?"

"I'll tell you what I tell the twins, all the time. 'Fair is a weather forecast.' That doesn't mean we won't win. You did one bang-up job and there have to be a lot of people out there questioning Finley's motives now. Dave's happy, Jess is slaphappy—"

"Because he finally took a painkiller! When he's rational again he'll realize he was right. I should've let him find a l—"

"Signey," Kelly interrupted. Her eyes, so like Jess's, were filled with disappointment. "He's not the I-told-you-so kind, even if he believed that. What's going on with you two, anyway?" Then she answered her own question. "You're in love with him."

"Yes. I love him."

"But?"

"I can't . . . I don't think I can be what he wants me to be, Kelly. When he got hurt in Cheyenne I thought I'd die. I couldn't hear anything, Kel. There was this awful silence in my head and I just left. I wasn't even

going to fly him out here until you called. I won't be
there next time, Kelly. I . . . can't be there again."

Jess had come into the living room, ready to crow
about beating Dave at pool, having used his cane for a
cue stick. His grin faded upon hearing Signey's last
words. Leaning heavily on the cane, he suddenly felt
the pain in his ankle begin to gnaw at him again.

Signey met his long, pain-filled look and couldn't
help wondering if she'd hurt him worse than the bull
had.

"Jess?" Kelly said. "Why don't you just admit you
could use another pain pill?"

"No." He ground out the refusal. He fixed Signey
with an almost threatening stare and limped closer.
"What I need is to talk to Signey."

Signey rose. "Talking won't help, Jess."

"*Not* talking sure as hell won't help."

Looking from one to other, Kelly started to get up
and leave. Jess touched a hand to her shoulder. "Stay
put, Kel. Signey and I'll go out for a walk." He limped
across the living room to the front door, then threw his
cane into the corner. "Are you coming, Signey?"

The words resounded again in her head. *Are you
coming, Signey? Or am I going to limp out of here
alone?* Every time she gave in to him, every time he
asked and she went along, she drew closer to the edge
of an emotional abyss.

Helpless to break the pattern, she was starting for
him when the phone rang. Dave had disappeared to the
shower, Kelly was nearly unable to move. Jess picked
up his cane, opened the door and walked out without
her, leaving her—to answer the phone? To follow him?

She answered, and immediately wished she'd gone out that door with Jess and let Kelly get to the phone when she could.

"This Signey Jensen?" the quiet, male voice asked.

"Yes."

"Carver, Ms. Jensen. Jimmy Carver," he supplied. "Heard your press conference this a.m. I've always been very much a fan of your style—nothing's changed about that."

"I . . . well, thank you. I appreciate that very much." Her initial surprise subsiding a little, Signey covered the mouthpiece and told Kelly who the caller was.

"Only one problem. You've got nothing but unhappy investors to back your man's story. What would you say to proof of tampering?"

Signey felt herself go very still. "You're speaking of real evidence—of proof that Dave's cars—?"

"I'm talking about John Cragen, darlin'. The dude's come out of the woodwork and wound up right here . . . in my office."

JESS PICKED HIS WAY around the deck surrounding his sister's house to the hot tub in back. There was no moon, just countless stars in the warm, enveloping darkness. He sat down on the edge of the tub, peeled the sock and Ace bandage off his throbbing ankle, turned on the jets and plunged his foot into the hot, turbulent water.

His plan had worked. Signey had found guts in herself to spare. She'd conducted that news conference as well as anyone he'd ever seen. In one decisive moment, she'd resigned from Cable Sports and made a powerful statement on Dave's behalf.

He wanted to find a way to translate that victory into another, more personal triumph. By giving up a niche she'd struggled hard to carve out for herself, she'd taken an unbelievable leap of faith in her own ability to land on her feet. He needed her to do the same with their relationship.

He finally understood her. He'd misread almost every cue. He'd set out to seduce her, physically and emotionally. Little had he realized that the seduction of Signey was and had always been the seduction of Hawkins. Physical intimacy in exchange for an emotional commitment.

She loved him. He knew that. It was the commitment she fought. In spite of everything he'd tried to teach her about his risks, the possibility that he'd get killed someday was a risk she wouldn't take.

He pulled his foot out for a second, measured the inevitable throbbing, then let it slide back into the water.

"Jess?"

Signey's voice washed over him as it always did, and he wondered if, sooner or later, he'd have to do without ever hearing it again. About now he'd give anything for a cigar. "Go back to the house, Signey."

She sat down on the redwood bench near him with her knees raised and her arms locked around them. "Don't you even want to know who called?"

The sight of her rounded shoulders, the sweet curve of her back . . . Would he have to go without that, too? He swallowed hard and looked away, to the starlight on the black, foaming water. "Not particularly."

"Jess, it was Jimmy Carver. . . . He's got John Cragen. He's got proof of tampering."

"Great." Jess's patience had worn as thin as the fine mist of moisture coming off the top of the tub.

Signey gave up. "What is it, Jess? Maybe you should get your ankle X-rayed?"

"I want to go home." Home. He knew now that home meant more than the ranch. More than a place.

"You'll be there tomorrow," she offered softly. "Or the next day. Carver wants us to see—"

"It's not that simple, babe. I want you there. I want to know you'll stay."

Signey laid her hands upon her knees and her head on top of them. Quiet desperation flooded her. Starlight silhouetted Jess in the darkness. "I'll stay, Hawkins. It's 'forever' I can't promise."

Lord, he wanted a cigar. It'd be so simple to get "forever" out of her. All he had to do was say, *"Okay, Signey, I'll quit bullfighting. I'll stay out of the arena."* And he could do it. He had no doubt that he could walk away from rodeo and like as not, never miss it. But he understood himself well enough to know that it was power he craved and control he needed. Tied so fundamentally to those needs, he'd just find some other way of fulfilling them. She wouldn't like that, either.

"Not good enough, babe."

Her throat tightened unbearably. "I need time, Jess. Perspective, maybe. Everything in my life has been turned upside down. Is it . . . is it too much to ask? Just a little time?"

"Time for what, Signey? To find a way to leave?"

"A way to stay, Jess. I . . . I want that, you know. I want to be able to st-stay."

The break in her voice shook him. He didn't have to see the stricken expression to know what it cost her to admit to the simple, binding truth of having fallen so far in love.

The simplest truth of all was that he had no choice and wouldn't take the way out if he had. If it was time she needed, time she'd have.

Time. He pulled his foot out, left his cane in favor of Signey's shoulder, and took the back way into the guest bedroom, to the bed with Kelly's Hands across America quilt.

He took Signey into his arms as he lay down again. A wind chime clinked gently in the night. Distant summer lightning illuminated the room for the length of a heartbeat. He kissed her, thinking time was all he had, anyway.

He nuzzled her throat and thought about protecting her for all time. He cupped her breast and thought about a child of theirs suckling her in time. He needed her feminine shape to complete himself, so touched the center of her sex, and in no time dragged a poignant cry of sweet pleasure from her.

He stroked her, and tremors rocked her body. He moved to enter her, then covered her instead. He touched his lips, his tongue to her breast, teasing her nipples to a point beyond pain and before fulfillment, to her stomach, to her thighs, to the secret parts of her and the deepest recesses in her body.

Time.

She willed the instant he filled her to last forever.

JIMMY CARVER stepped out of a limo onto the curb near the Las Vegas Convention Center, followed by two bodyguards. He held a cigar in one hand and had a bulging, oversize briefcase chained to his other wrist.

Powerfully built, a Cree Indian by descent, his voice deeper than Jess's baritone, he stood a full head shorter than Signey. Following her gaze to the chain at his wrist, he explained. "Some very...sensitive material here."

They stood, Signey with Jess, Dave and Kelly, at the entrance to Carver's offices. His guards waited discreetly behind him while he sent off his driver with a curt nod, then turned a smile on Signey. "So, little lady, you've taken the tiger by the tail again, haven't you?"

She laughed, somehow put instantly at ease by his calling her a little lady, when he stood only shoulder high to her. "I guess you could say that. You know Dave, of course?"

Carver turned and gave Dave an appraising once-over. "Dave. Got a soft spot in my heart for the hometown boys.... Only a little the worse for wear and tear, to all appearances."

Dave gripped the proffered hand. "No thanks to Finley."

Carver turned to Kelly. "And is this your lovely wife?"

Kelly offered him her hand and in turn introduced Jess.

"Ah, the inimitable Hawkins." Carver's probing eyes encompassed them all. "Shall we get to it?"

His suite of offices pitted a lush decor against an enormous, battered, government-issue desk. There were computer-enhanced video capabilities at one end of the fifty-foot room, countered by old-fashioned black chalkboards at the other. Signey studied the statistics Carver collected in a dozen colors of chalk scribbling and grew truly impressed. The man's prowess outdid his reputation. Las Vegas covered any bet anyone wanted to lay on any event. Carver provided the odds.

Unlocking the guard chain at his wrist, he caught Signey in an undulgent smile. "Something amuses you, Signey?"

"All the cloak-and-dagger—"

He took the videotape—about twice as thick as a home VCR tape—from his briefcase. "Make no mistake, Signey Jensen. What you've begun here is no cloak-and-dagger weekend getaway, no music video cops and robbers. You want to play with the big boys, the first thing you do is protect your ass, the second is, protect your goods. Got it?"

The intensity in his eyes almost frightened her. She drew a deep breath and nodded. "I'm afraid I don't, Carver. What have you got?"

Carver shoved a half-dozen-deep bank of chalkboards to one side, inserted the videotape into the wall-resident video unit and picked up a remote control.

Signey sat forward on the couch beside Jess as the tape began to roll.

"Let me show you what we can do here first. Then, Dave, I'll show you exactly how your wheels were sabotaged."

He let the tape run for a few seconds, then sped it up, brought the pace to slow motion, and finally cut it down to frame by frame. Dave's car inched along. Carver picked a frame in which the Christmas tree of lights appeared, then activated a computer-assisted close-up.

Signey looked at Jess, couldn't believe the technology she was seeing. Each close-up, Carver explained, magnified the picture by a factor of ten, until an unilluminated, amber lamp in the sequence of starting lights filled the screen. The texture and color reproduction reminded Signey of a honeycomb.

Dave swore softly under his breath. "Carver, what are you doing with high-tech stuff like this?"

"Man, that's like asking a bird what it's doing with wings!" Carver groused good-naturedly. "You want to fly, you've got to have wings. You want to make odds, you better know your stuff. Now look at this. . . ."

Carver advanced the tape, then chose extremely fine magnification and flicked through the frames one by one; the gloved hands of the pit crew were working on one of the wheels. Carver froze the frame where the deadly sabotage occurred. Dave sucked in a shocked breath. Signey had no idea what she was looking at, but apparently Dave did. "That's it, sports fans," he murmured.

"Premeditated as hell," Jess said quietly.

The three men launched into a discussion of welds and lug nuts and road torque meaningless to Signey. But she'd been right from the beginning. "Why would anybody do this if they knew the videotapes were running?"

"Interesting angle, Signey," Carver said. "Just what I wanted to know. But you've got to figure this from Finley's viewpoint. Long as he's ordered the sabotage, he might as well have insurance that the boys doin' the job will keep their mouths shut. If we back off from this magnification, everyone of those guys can be identified—not by us, but by each other."

"What's the bottom line, Carver?" Signey asked, her stomach churning angrily. "Who's responsible?"

"You can't tell from this, Sig—"

"Cragen's your man, Dave," Carver interrupted smoothly.

"Cragen admitted to *this?*" Signey cried.

Dave took one look at Kelly's stricken face and shot out of his chair. "I'll kill the son of a—"

"Sit down, Lindstrom," Carver ordered, "and listen for a minute." Dave did neither, but continued to pace the length of the room, walking the edge of a deep, violent anger.

Carver went on, anyway. "Cragen has agreed to go state's evidence against Finley and friends in exchange for immunity. The way he tells it, he was being blackmailed, he did the deeds, he took the videotapes and planned to vanish. Only thing stopping him, Signey, was your press conference. You broke the ice on this treacherous little pond, and Cragen knew he'd have to turn himself in."

"Makes sense," Jess agreed, his own temper reflected in the disdainful set of his jaw and the shiny whiteness of his scar. "My question is, how did you wind up with a copy?"

Carver smiled enigmatically. "I never fool with the odds and I wouldn't tamper with the evidence. On the other hand, I saw a moral imperative in making sure said evidence survives. I ran a duplicate last night before Cragen handed it over to the cops."

If Signey had been impressed with Carver before, she was now awed by him. His action insured that Finley's influence couldn't destroy that tape.

"Meanwhile, Cragen is compelled to testify," Carver said, "for whatever that's worth. I should think nailing Finley makes the tradeoff worth a great deal." He punched in a number on his speakerphone, then asked for homicide division, Detective Lucero. Put on hold for a minute, he looked from Dave to Signey. "Lucero is waiting to hear from you." Addressing both of them, he asked, "You two sure you're up to this?"

10

ON A MONDAY AFTERNOON seven weeks later, when Signey had begun to feel restive and alone because Jess had been fishing since dawn, Ken Webb called. He'd quit Cable Sports and had just received an offer from a highly respected San Francisco television station. His news hit her wrong, like an innocent rap on a funny bone.

Where was *her* new job? Seven weeks later, shouldn't she have been thinking about looking? And why hadn't she missed it before this?

Confused by her reaction, Signey forced herself into the appropriate response to Ken's news. "California goes home! Congratulations, Ken! Really. When do you start?"

"They want me on board by the time the Grand Nationals start at the Cow Palace."

"More rodeo. Aren't you the lucky one!" Signey crowed.

"Yeah, I just keep getting luckier and luckier. How about you? Your phone ringing off the hook with job offers?"

Signey laughed. Wasn't that what a person was supposed to do with a hurt funny bone? "Not exactly."

"Well, you're not exactly out there beating the bushes, either."

"No. I'm ... vacationing."

"Vacation? Come off it, Signey. You're the worst workaholic—"

"Stow it, Webb."

"Or what, sweetstuff? Another golf tourney?"

She touched her earlobe where Jess always did, then jerked her hand away. "Sorry, Ken. Old habits die hard, I guess. I must just be a little on edge."

"You must be enjoying yourself, sweetstuff, or you wouldn't still be there. What's got you so on edge?"

"I . . . it has been wonderful, Ken. I could get used to this."

"Oh, well. That clears things right up for me," Ken cracked. "What, for instance?"

My half of Jess's bed. And the way Jess had of looking at her. The look that said, *"Everything I have is yours for the taking."*

But such things were impossible to explain to Ken, so she promised to get her head on straight real soon, and phone him up when she'd managed that.

But that wasn't the end of the subject. How was it possible that she'd gone seven weeks without thinking twice about her future?

Because.

Because, outside her own professional goals, everything Jess had was everything she'd ever wanted. He was not a poor man. He owned the ranchland his father had initially carved out—a property a man could ride over for three days and not be done.

He'd built a spectacular glass-fronted house at the edge of a lake a man could row half the day and not reach the other side.

The house had five bedrooms, and he'd built it without knowing the woman he might bring to it one day, without dreaming of the baby feet that might tread its floors. Until now.

He could ride his ranch, fish his streams, row his boat, even occupy his house. But a man alone couldn't furnish his house with babies.

That was it. She'd begun to think she wanted nothing more than babies with Jess.

There had been signs, times when Jess had started talking babies, no matter how obliquely. He'd set out to offer her everything he had, and a heartbreaker of a smile always chased the look that said, *"Mi casa es su casa."* Ever and always, Hawkins had a line and smile. She lived for those smiles, those lines.

For the past seven weeks nothing had existed for Signey but Jess and the family and a trip to town every once in awhile. The nightlife was spectacular, the shopping cosmopolitan and the living easy.

So easy.

Faking the possibility of forever had never been as simple as now, while Jess stayed away from rodeo, allowing his ankle to heal.

She could get used to this life. She'd begun thinking of this side of the closet and that side of the bed as hers. She'd grown accustomed to the twins' "Aunt Sig." When Cammie asked Jess what a French kiss was, he told her that was when people opened their mouths to kiss. When Cammie asked if anybody really did that, Jess said yes. And when Cammie asked if Signey really was her aunt, Jess cleared his throat and told the child Signey would always be her aunt. To him, one truth was as simple as the next.

Times like that, Signey hurt almost more than she could stand. If Jess had forgotten, she hadn't. The image of him caught on the horns of that bull—the sight of his ankle every day—reminded her why she could never have this man. She wasn't strong enough.

She wanted always to be there for Cammie as an aunt might be, but it'd have to be as a maiden aunt, and she told Hawkins so. He just smiled and Signey just chilled a little every time he smiled like that.

A week ago, she'd stumbled upon a conversation between Jess and his mother.

"Victoria..."

"I'm your mother," she'd snapped, "not some interfering old biddy you can address by her first name like that."

"But you are interfering, Mother. We're consenting adults, and when we're ready to get married, we will. In the meantime, kindly butt out."

She announced her presence and set them both straight. She had no intention of getting married.

Victoria clearly wasn't any better at listening than her son. "Signey, dear, when is your birthday, anyway?"

"February," she'd returned. "Which has nothing—"

"To do with anything," Victoria blithely interrupted, "except that you're not getting any younger, my dear. In labor and delivery—you know I was a delivery nurse in my younger days? Anyway, you're already what is known as an 'elderly prima gravida,' meaning..."

Signey knew what it meant. *Old* for having a first baby. "I'm not marrying, and I'm not having babies...." This she'd said despite the facts. She'd never wanted anything more in her life than Jess's babies....

The phone rang again, disturbing her reverie. It was Victoria with an invitation for dinner. Thinking of the trout Jess intended to grill for the two of them that night, Signey hesitated. Victoria dashed into the tiny crack of Signey's pause. "Of course you will come. I'll be expecting you around seven. Would you mind, Signey dear, thawing some of those spectacular rolls of yours?" Victoria didn't take no for an answer any more than Jess did.

Signey wandered into the kitchen, resentfully pulled a bag of rolls from the freezer, than began to brew coffee. The phone rang for a third time.

She yanked out a stool from under the breakfast bar in the kitchen, plunked herself down and answered again. "Grand Central Station!"

"Really? Guess I must have the wrong number," teased a husky base voice. Carver.

"No, not really. It's a paradise up here. How's life in the big city?"

"Too fast, as usual. Suits the hell out of me, though. Might want to turn on the news tonight. Do they allow television in paradise?"

"This one, anyway. Big screen, even. We haven't turned it on in a long time."

"Try it," Carver suggested. "You'll be on tonight. They've just announced the grand jury indictments out against Finley *et al.*"

Finley had been indicted. Signey waited for the surge of victory, the satisfaction, but it never came. She nagged at herself for not feeling elated. How could she? How could she not?

"Signey? Are you still there?" Carver asked.

"Yes. Sure. That's great, Carver. The wheels of justice . . ."

"Yeah. Finley will be ground exceedingly fine."

"Nothing more than he deserves," she responded. "Carver?"

"Yeah?"

"You're around the convention center a lot. Do you ever hear of any openings at the news bureau?" Carver must be shocked to hear her asking, but Signey knew exactly where it'd come from. She needed to be busy again, busy enough to keep from wanting.... "I mean, a person's got to do something."

His hesitation fairly shouted at her. "Actually, I think they are looking to add a sports marketing position to the bureau directorship. Is that anything you'd be interested in?"

"Are you kidding me? Carver, that would be... perfect! Ideal." She could use all the contacts she'd nurtured over the years in the world of professional sports. She'd need to travel, negotiating deals to bring major sporting events to Las Vegas. She'd be too busy to miss the man or to think about the babies she would never have with him.

"But you know," Carver was saying, "the national press hounds are already licking their chops over the potential donnybrook between you and Dave and the guys in the black hats. Some even want odds on the outcome. Some news rag will probably offer a fortune for an exclusive from you. Set you up for life."

Ask Jess, Carver. I'm already set for life. Name the subject, object or need, and Jess is there to fill it. All but one. He can't help being the man he is. "Carver? Tell the bureau director I'll be down to talk about the sports marketing position, will you?"

"Will do. Tune into the tube. You oughta be on soon."

Signey thought seriously about ignoring the television, but couldn't, and turned on the set. The final "Jeopardy" answer was being posed in the category of astronomy.

"Literally," said the game-show host, "the meaning of 'aurora borealis.'"

"Northern dawn," Signey answered absently. As in the North Star, itself a lodestar. Like the design on the mirror Paul had given her so she wouldn't cry anymore.

Startled, she realized she hadn't thought of her mirror in weeks. Never a day had gone by, before Jess, that she hadn't touched her mirror or thought of it, even if she hadn't needed it. Was life so good here with Jess that she had no need of an emotional crutch? Or was this life merely stifling? No challenge left or need to fake it, no stress, no mirror. No Signey.

She switched stations, and seven commercials later, the Reno station news came on with its lead story. "Big news out of Carson City today. The grand jury announced multiple bills of indictment against Cable Sports tycoon, Walter D. Finley, owner of Cable Sports and the majority owner of cars in the championship auto racing teams driven by Nevada's own Dave Lindstrom. Based on information obtained from Lindstrom, an anonymous source and ex-Cable Sports reporter Signey Jensen . . ."

Ex-reporter Signey Jensen. The tag should have slammed into her, hard. Perhaps the prospect of a position in Las Vegas sports marketing took the sting from this moment.

Signey pressed the on-off button of the remote control. She should have been wild with joy over the news of Finley's demise and angry as hell over the "ex-reporter" remarks. Silence filled the big house, and Signey finally understood the cause of her muted reactions. Nothing mattered to her anymore as much as Jess.

For weeks his family had cast her in wholly new roles. Cammie and Danny wanted an aunt. A real aunt. Victoria saw in her a reluctant daughter-in-law, Dave an in-law ally, Kelly a sister. She could be this child's aunt, that child's mother, Mrs. Hawkins.

Mrs. Inimitable Hawkins.

Instead she would go back to work. And the moment she went back, Jess would go back—to being who and what *he* was. A risk taker. And that would be the end of Signey and Jess.

Especially not this one. The fear would never go away.

JESS HIKED DOWN from the stream he'd fished, congratulating himself on the fact that his ankle was nearly back to full strength. From the back door he saw Signey curled up, resting her head on the arm of the sofa. He put his creel into one side of the kitchen sink and washed his hands in the other, then walked into the living room and knelt beside her.

He kissed her. God, he'd never get tired of touching her, tasting, teasing.

Signey drew a ragged breath. His kiss felt so good. Always felt so good.

Something hesitant in her expression caught at him. "Wanna come check out your dinner? Pretty fine catch, if I do say so myself."

She opened her eyes, then looked away. "We're going to Victoria's for dinner."

"No. We're not. Not tonight, anyway."

"Yes, Jess. We are. She called a little while ago, insisting. Barbecued ribs and corn, she said. Jess's favorites. What could I say?"

Jess sank back on the floor and sat Indian style. "No. Did you try no?"

"I'm not good at no, Jess. She's your mother," Signey flared, rising from the sofa. "You tell her no." She tossed the TV's remote control onto the end table and fled the living room to go change for dinner.

Jess followed a few seconds later. Signey stripped off her shirt and cutoffs and tried to ignore him. She was being bitchy and shrewish, but how could she say it was the coming end of their relationship that had her so moody and skittish?

"What's that supposed to mean?"

"Just what I said. Tell her yourself."

"I mean the part about your not being good at no." His voice was calm, but his eyes flashed uneasily.

"Nothing." If she'd been any good at no, she'd have used her ticket to Cheyenne instead of flying with him. "I'm dressing for dinner at your mother's."

"The trout—"

"Dammit, Hawkins, I don't want trout. I don't like trout, I don't like fish."

He grabbed her wrist and stripped the fresh blouse out of her hand. "Since when?"

She glared at him and jerked away, then turned to the closet for another blouse. There wasn't one. She went scarlet for no reason, felt heat exploding upward from her breasts. Without turning around, she asked for her clothing back.

He saw the flush on her skin, felt her raw embarrassment and swore at himself for humiliating her.

She forced herself to face him. "Just...can I have my blouse back, please?"

He held it out to her. She reached for it. He held on and didn't know he did. She held one sleeve and couldn't seem to take it away.

His voice grew hoarse, and his green eyes filled with confusion. "What is it? What's wrong, babe?"

"For one thing, my name is Signey, Jess. Not Aunt Sig, not plain Sig, and not babe."

Like the time she'd left her come-hither dress hanging in her closet, Jess felt as if he'd been kicked in the chest. "I see." He dropped his end of her blouse. Turning on his heel, he left the room.

THEY DROVE to the main ranch house for dinner. Any other night they would have walked, sharing the time. Tonight the prolonged silence between them would have been unbearable.

The celebration at Victoria's was in full swing. Signey felt shame streaking through her and flushed again. She'd been so caught up in her own crisis that she hadn't even passed on the news of the indictments to Jess.

"Didn't you guys hear?" Dave demanded. Of course they'd heard. Carver had called Signey. The indictments were all over the national news. The grand jury! Finley! Justice would be done now, and Dave would be vindicated. Jess forced a broad smile and clapped Dave on the shoulder in congratulation.

"Didn't you tell Jess, Sig? Carver said he called you, too." It took the family, Signey thought, about thirty seconds to figure it out.

Victoria filled the awkward moment with a curt if bewildered, "Dinner's on the table."

But the awkwardness lingered. Only Cammie and Danny's chatter, along with baby Jason's antics, made the atmosphere bearable at all. Signey picked at the ribs on her plate and kept silent. Finally Victoria asked Signey what Carver had said to her.

Kelly dabbed at the toddler's sticky chin and scooped bits of mashed corn from the tray of his high chair. "Oh, Mother, just forget it. Finley will get what he deserves. I think we should all just forget and forgive and get on with our lives."

Plainly taken aback, Victoria glared at her. "I don't know where you got that Goodie-Two-Shoes attitude, Kelly. Certainly none of my doing!"

"Actually," Signey interjected, a little too brightly, even to her own ears, "he said there might be a place for me at the convention center. Sports marketing. I'm flying down tomorrow to talk with them."

"Sig, that's great!" Dave offered. And Kelly smiled broadly, about to offer her congratulations, as well.

As far as Jess was concerned, Signey might as well have kicked him where it counted most. His shock instantly ruled the reaction around the table. Six pairs of eyes fled from Jess's wrath, stared at Signey, and then fixed firmly on six plates, avoiding the end of the table where Jess sat. The ear of corn he held dropped.

Signey clumsily dunked her shaking fingertips into the finger bowl and upset it. She had no idea where the decision to fly to Vegas had come from, or when. Did it even matter? Knowing she'd landed a blow below the belt, she lifted her chin. "I'd like to take the Bonanza, if that's all right with you."

"Go to hell if you like, *babe*. But not in my bird."

11

"JESS, FOR GOD'S SAKE! The kids!" Victoria hissed.

Kelly and Dave turned at once to pull back Cammie and Danny's chairs. Both scampered away without so much as a hint of resistance.

Signey barely noticed. Her face flamed. The heat spread everywhere in her body. Silence roared in her ears, and bitter recriminations that were only partly true popped out of her mouth.

"I see now! Everything yours is mine for the taking—the Bonanza, the ranch, the house, the goldfish and the kids—if I stay put, barefoot and pregnant. Isn't that right, Jess? And oh, I forgot! There's fresh trout for dinner, if I can only learn to say no to your mother."

"Dammit, Signey, that's pure bull and you know it."

"Is it? Which part, Jess?"

Dave intervened. "Jess, Sig, c'mon. Quit before you really blow it all to hell, huh?"

She'd forgotten Dave, forgotten Kelly and Victoria. Swallowing a leaden lump in her throat, Signey reached to touch Victoria's stricken, shaking hand. "I'm sorry, Victoria. I didn't mean to ruin your dinner. I mean... I'm sorry." She rose and walked out.

The screen on the front door banged. Jess shoved back his chair, strode out of the dining room and into his father's den without a backward glance.

The door to the den, too, slammed behind him with a taunting finality. Reaching for the brandy decanter on the shelf next to the Louis L'Amour and Hemingway classics, Jess poured himself a shot glass full and lit a cigar out of his father's humidor. Pacing like a half-starved mountain lion confronted with a baited trap, he gulped the brandy in a single swallow and slammed down the glass on the old, scarred cherry-wood desk.

The heat spread downward from his throat. Lord, how he missed the old man . . . dead just eight months now. How he missed Signey, gone maybe eight minutes.

Kelly came in without knocking and clung to the doorknob behind her as she leaned against the door for support.

Jess stopped short in his pacing, then spun away. "Don't start, Kel. I don't know where she came up with that crap, but I sure as hell—"

"Go home, Jess. Make it right before it's too late."

He'd been prepared for an argument, maybe because he knew Kelly would be the last one to mince words with him. Desperation clawed like talons at his throat; he was ready to kick something in. "I don't know how to make it right, Kel. I've said it all." He rubbed at his thigh, the damaged muscle still ached when he became tired or tense. "I can't bully her into seeing things my way and I can't give her enough to make up for what she's lost."

"You aren't angry about the job, are you?"

"No. It isn't the job."

"Does she know that?"

"Yeah. She knows."

Tears formed in Kelly's eyes and spilled down her cheek, spattering a damp, crazy pattern on her maternity smock. Jess looked for a long moment at his sister's gently rounded abdomen and yearned desperately, impossibly for simpler, easier times. Times when all a woman knew to want was what a man could offer. Maybe he'd been born a century or so too late.

He reached out to Kelly and wiped away another tear. "Signey doesn't cry. Did you know?"

"Never?"

"Never."

Kelly stroked his cheek, offering sibling comfort in the same easy manner she had of telling him where to get off when he needed that. "Can you stand just one more pregnant lady observation?"

"Maybe one, Kel," he answered wearily.

"If she doesn't cry, well, it's…maybe it's like the dry heaves, Jess. Nothing really happens, but it still hurts real bad."

SIGNEY STOOD RIGIDLY before the window seat in Jess's bedroom, staring out at the peaceful, unrippled surface of the lake. The moon shone brilliantly and filled the room with its reflected light while her eyes filled with unspent tears. She had a cold, leaden lump in place of her heart, and there seemed no way to warm up. Gathering a blanket from the chest by the window, she pulled it around her shoulders.

She felt despicable for having forgotten to tell Jess about the indictments and disloyal for throwing the position at the news bureau at him in front of his family. But more than anything she felt miserable. Jess re-

fused to recognize the feelings she could never escape—
the panic she felt every time she saw his faded bruises
and remembered.... *Especially not this one.*

She drew the blanket closer, recalling poignant moments, quiet moments, crazy moments. And times so
intensely sexual that she felt again the heated tension
rising in her. But all they had that was good couldn't
outweigh what might happen in the space of a heartbeat; her terror was reflexive, involuntary and terribly, terribly personal.

Having no frame of reference, no real experience with
terror, Jess could never understand. The job in Vegas
was her chance to walk away from him. Telling him as
she had, with no warning, was just her cowardly way
of getting through to him.

Signey turned away from the window, back into the
bedroom. Opening the chest again, she pulled out a
pillow and turned to go lie on the sofa. Jess stood silhouetted against the doorjamb.

He'd been there in the dark for a long time, thinking
about pain and about tears and hurts that wouldn't go
away. His bedroom held the barest scents of a woman,
of Signey. If he buried his nose in his own pillow, he'd
smell hyacinth. He could almost hear her saying he
couldn't understand, would never understand why his
loving wasn't enough for her.

She was right.

He started to speak, but for some stupid reason the
words stuck. "Wouldn't it—?" He cleared his throat and
looked away from her, staring at her knitting needles
atop his bedding chest, covered with baby-pink yarn for

Kelly's new one. He swallowed hard and began again. "Wouldn't it be easier to cry than to run?"

Yes. Anything would be easier than leaving him. Almost anything. But though his question was gently voiced, the emotion behind it was as volatile as lightning-struck tinder and she clutched the pillow to her breast. All she could see of his eyes were the white parts glittering in the darkness, but she felt him staring at her from top to toe. Her heart began to thud painfully, but before she could think of some way to answer him the phone rang.

He swore under his breath, let it ring half a dozen times, then finally answered.

He listened for awhile without saying a thing. Then, "Yeah, this is Hawkins."

His eyes searched out Signey's and held. "Yeah. Okay. I'll be there." Three fingers of one hand jammed into his Levi's, he flipped the receiver away from his shoulder and let it fall into place, all without breaking eye contact with her.

The call back to the rodeo arena had come at last, and with such exquisitely awful timing.

She knew. She recognized the silent challenge. Hawkins would go back to bullfighting. She stared at him, and he stared at her, but he wouldn't blink first. She looked away.

Long, silent moments passed before he expelled yet another frustrated breath. "This is not about your taking any job. You know that, don't you?" he asked softly.

"Where are you going?"

"Pendleton. Oregon. I have to get on with my life, too, babe, but I'm talking about Vegas, about your job.

Tell me you know this tension between us has nothing to do with a job."

"All right! Yes! This is about more of a relationship than I've ever been ready for. This is about taking one quick peek over a cliff and deciding the rappel looks like a whole lot of fun and not half so treacherous as it seems."

She threw the pillow onto the bed she had shared with him for the last two months. "I don't even want to watch, Hawkins, but I won't stand in your way." Pain like acid ate through her stomach, but she had to do this. The time had long since passed for cutting him loose. Her voice never wavered, even when he started for her.

Even when he stood two thin inches away and she was forced to look up to make him hear.

"You thought faking it would do. You thought if you could just show me how awfully good you are, I could let it go." Her voice threatened to break. "This is no little thing Jess, no Band-Aid fix-up. The problem, you see—" her voice broke "—is . . . is that I know exactly how good you are and exactly how much I have to lose."

Barbed wire was gentler to a deer's tender flesh than the injury ripping through Jess. If he were another kind of man she'd have no problems, no need even of Band-Aids.

He wasn't another kind of man, and if he had been, she'd never have fallen for him in the first place.

It occurred to him that he'd never taken her feelings seriously, that he'd pushed and shoved in all the wrong places. Instead of drawing her nearer, he'd driven her away. And he was angry.

He'd never begun to guess how deep her scars ran. He'd tried to transform her fears into something manageable, and only managed to dig himself a deeper hole. Even as his lips touched hers, he knew he was wrong. He was too down-in-the-gut angry at having been wrong, at having dazzled her with strength and prowess and then expected her to believe his mastery exempted him from harm.

He was only a man and an angry one, and his lips on hers were hard and too intemperate. Signey stiffened like a threatened doe. And just as quickly her lips under his answered in kind, intemperate and exacting the price she paid. Her comeback did nothing for his self-control.

The kiss lasted until neither one of them could breathe. He broke away, and Signey looked away, but he wouldn't let that happen. He'd told her she could go to hell, but he hadn't meant that. He knew that was what she'd wanted—to bait him, inveigle him into walking out . . . because she didn't have the strength to leave him on her own.

In the dark her eyes were luminous, shadowed and overlarge. He would have killed for the grace of a single tear, then the foolish woman's lip trembled. The mirror had never taught her how to contain that dead giveway, and it damn near broke him.

"Listen," she begged.

"I hear you."

"Don't make this harder."

"It can't get harder."

"Then let me go, before—"

She looked to him as fragile as the first spring flower in a bank of snow, and he shook his head. No. "Not in this lifetime."

"Jess . . ."

He was done with words. She could see that clearly, just as she saw the danger in defying him another minute. He clamped his lips down hard upon hers as he lifted her, blanket, body and soul and carried her the six feet to the side of his bed. He knew, *knew* how absolutely, incontrovertibly impossible this thing between them was, and he was in no mood for it.

He laid her down and stood to strip off his shirt and tear at his button-down jeans.

She was just reckless enough to defy him. Her voice was low and insistent. "I don't think this will change—"

"That's your whole problem, Signey. You think too damn much." Her flannel nightgown hit the floor in no time at all, then his shorts, and in no more time than any of that had taken he came down on top of her.

If she thought he would seduce her, she was wrong. If she thought he would indulge her in the luxuries of time and moisture, tempo and anticipation, she was wrong. He wanted her beyond reason. Reason was what was destroying her. He gathered her hands, pinned them above her head, and buried himself in her.

The stinging in her became something exquisitely pleasurable, something explosive before the shock ever registered. Her body reacted just as frantically, her nipples tensed and ached as quickly, and her shoulders drew back to lever her hips toward him, meeting him more than halfway.

With Jess she'd known loving like winter sunshine, like fireworks on the Fourth of July, like a bonfire on a cold autumn night. This was wildfire, driven and consuming. She was as much the cause of the fury as its willful victim.

Signey's body spoke to him, recklessly clamping around him, drawing him in deeper. She bucked toward him, giving more, demanding more, and he praised her body's response and careless abandon; when her body spoke for her, he heard something more powerful than intellect or emotion. Something irreducible.

Love.

When the terrible need to take her subsided, others grew out of the ashes and bloomed as wildflowers will in the wake of a fire storm. Still within her, Jess began anew the seduction of Signey. His lips touched hers and molded themselves there until he had to breathe. His tongue wandered and streaked down her neck, over the breastbone guarding her heart, her nipples rising so sassily, so needily to his tongue.

Now she was beyond careful reason and contrivance.

At last he released her hands, and her fingers threaded into his hair. She held him to her breast because the tension there was unbearably sweet, unbelievably painful, intimately tied to the spasms rocking her womb, seizing him.

His wild, potent response granted her every power and filled her with wanton, erotic acts of abandon. Her past was barren of fulfillment like this, and the prospect of her future without Jess was just as bleak.

They would have this one last night. Whether he wanted to believe it or not, loving him and living with the only kind of man he could be were as disparate as sun and moon. Tonight she would give him all she had in her to give.

Jess knew his game, his bid to win her was nearly a draw. He'd baited her, raised the ante, dealt her every wild card. He'd stuck with her like a man dispossessed of his smarts every time she had tried to push him away. He'd rolled with her in ankle-deep mud and kissed her until she was silly and magical steam came out his ears.

Now he rolled onto his back to accommodate her overtures. She stroked and tasted and touched, and when she brushed her lips against the juncture of thigh and body, he went again from willow soft to oak hard and groaned with the pleasure. The second time for him was always more difficult, always more exquisite, had always more of forever.

When she believed he couldn't stand another second, Signey hesitated for one more; no one loved a gambit better than Jess.

He smiled because her brazen mischief pleased him, then the smile died. He knew no woman could ever love him half as much as she did, and his whisper was grating, rasp-file harsh. "Can you think I'll ever let you go, babe?"

She smiled at him, but her smile waned, as well, for she knew no woman could ever have been so ill-equipped to love a man like him so much.

He pulled her down over him, and the dark, velvety upward strokes undid her. "Never, Signey. Never."

IN THE MORNING Jess saw her off to Vegas in his Bonanza, certain she'd be back by nightfall. Instead he got a phone call. The convention authority wanted her, it seemed, and she needed to stay over to commit the details to a contract in the morning.

"That's great, babe."

Jess wanted her, too, and though he wanted to be happy for her, he couldn't help resenting Signey's quick and easy commitment. So he didn't say much at all beyond letting her know he wouldn't need the plane to make Pendleton until the day after. "Take your time."

Wasn't that what she'd asked for? Time?

He sat at his kitchen table, listening to her other news, leaning back with his feet up. But his neck was tighter than a drawn bow as he listened to Signey hundreds of miles away.

"Carver pulled some strings and managed to get Dave an immediate appointment at Methodist Hospital in Minneapolis. They've got a fine sports-medicine reputation, and Carver thinks they'll be able to prove Dave's reflexes and coordination and stamina were never the problem Finley claims they were."

Jess wished he could be tested, too. Wouldn't it just be swell to hand Signey the results and erase all her fears? Pleased though he was for bankable evidence Dave could take to the trial, Jess couldn't help the resentment edging up a notch.

Nor could he help baiting her. "What do you think the tests will prove?"

"That Dave is as proficient and in shape as he ever was. That—"

"So you think a jury of twelve rational people will be able to look at numbers and graphs and charts and conclude that a man is able to do his job without getting himself killed." What he really wanted to know was how in hell she could believe in his brother-in-law—*how the hell* she could believe in scribbling on a piece of paper—without believing in him.

He knew the comparison wasn't fair. Believing in Dave presented Signey with no real emotional threat. Jess knew she knew exactly what he was really asking. It was a cheap shot and he knew it, but then, what else could he say?

How about "I love you," jerk? he carped at himself. *A simple "I love you."*

HER MEETING went well. The convention authority had begun to map out a strong program for courting the producers of bigger and better sporting events, aiming to lure them to Vegas.

Signey's recent notoriety accordingly became a definite plus, and hiring her a mere formality by the time her interviews were over the second morning. It should have done her heart more good than harm, except that she understood exactly what she was doing. Taking one step after another, away from Jess. Farther and farther afield with every clause in her agreement.

She told herself that she didn't taste the shrimp salad because of her excitement at the opportunities she would have. If her ground check of the Bonanza was cursory, she assured herself she could have performed the rote procedure in her sleep. If she had anything on her mind as she flew Jess's plane back to Reno, it was not her contract, not her future, but Jess.

She was prepared to believe the test results Methodist Hospital would generate as proof of Dave's mental and physical acuity. Numbers, ratios and conclusions drawn, the truth was that Signey believed in Dave and needed none of the scientific hocus-pocus.

But then, she wasn't in love with Dave Lindstrom. She was so deeply in love with Hawkins that the decision to walk away from him was only a little less devastating than watching him ripped away from her. But how did one compare heartache to heartbreak?

She flew home and spotted Jess standing at the far end of his private landing strip. She never noticed the indicator light that failed to come on when she activated the landing gear, never realized through the sorrow in her that she didn't hear the functioning of the gears when the wheels should have dropped, never made the crucial connection in her mind....

Until Jess, signaling frantically with repeated, wild, sweeping gestures, suddenly created confusion. Terror bit into her.

Instinct kicked in, taking over from her numbed mind, struggling to make up for her lapses. The split second that followed expanded in some crazy warp of time. She realized that she was about to bend Jess's bird—the pilot lingo for a forced landing came as naturally to her as breathing.

Jess looked so...angry. Signey knew she had to veer, had to take the bird off the landing strip. She'd already cut her speed until it was too late, far too late to power a lift, and far better to scrape the underbelly in the meadow grasses.

The Bonanza hit the end of the runway at an angle and with an incredible jolt, bounced and skidded crazily into the meadow. The prop caught, bit into the earth and broke off.

Cut off the power. She reached automatically to cut off the systems that might otherwise ignite a horrendous explosion. The tail of the Bonanza sank heavily to the ground.

She'd have been okay but for the briefcase flying through the cabin that slammed into the back of her head.

SIGNEY FLOATED in and out of consciousness for hours afterward. She heard the doctor talking somewhere above her head, ordering lab tests. Huge overhead lamps lit the emergency room and cast confusing shadows. She blinked, angry and confused at the tiny beam of light aimed at her pupils, and pulled away from the tight band being applied to her arm, jerked when a needle jab followed. Wavering, floating blackness.

Motion. Rolling. A cart? A needle, this time at her spine. She wanted to protest, wanted to say she just needed to sleep. Why wouldn't they just go away and leave her alone? *Jess, make them go away. Nightmare. Just a nightmare. Jess.*

Dr. Greenlee called Jess in from the waiting room and began asking questions.

"How old is Ms. Jensen?"

"Thirty-four," Jess answered mechanically.

"And how experienced at piloting?"

"I don't know. . . . Several hundred hours, maybe."

"No reason to think she shouldn't have been aware of the landing-gear failure . . . ?" Jess shook his head wearily, and Greenlee continued. "Any eating disorders that would cause her to black out? Diabetic?"

"No. Nothing like that." Jess hated hospitals, avoided doctors, and despised the sterile, but-those-are-the-rules mentality.

"Pregnant?"

"No!" All he could think about was Signey pregnant. Signey rounded with an infant of his body, her breasts swollen and heavy in his hands. The emptiness in him for doubting any of that would ever happen was worse than all the purely physical pain he'd ever known.

Shut out for so long while Greenlee pinched and prodded and took his X-rays, having made a pain in the ass of himself in the waiting room, now Jess couldn't seem to follow the simplest statement. Signey looked so pale, so fragile on that gurney. . . .

"Spinal fluid is clear, Mr. Hawkins. We'll send it up to the lab for a red-cell count, but I'm betting there is no intracranial hemorrhage—no bleeding. I think we're dealing with a concussion. I'd like to admit her for overnight observation."

"I'm taking her home. I can watch her better than any three of you."

Visibly impatient now, the doctor sighed heavily. "Mr. Hawkins, you have left me in absolutely no doubt as to your opinions. Or that you think you're up to watching over Miss Jensen. But you're not, and if you take her out of here with even the slightest chance she'll bleed into her head, it'll be AMA."

No nice euphemisms, just bleeding into her head.

And AMA. Jess knew that one. Against Medical Advice. He'd checked out of enough emergency rooms AMA himself to know it well. But this was different. This was Signey. "I'm staying with her," he warned.

"Fine. Stay with her, sit with her, I don't care if you sleep with her, but stay the hell out of my way."

Jess did two of the three, sat with her through the night and kept out of Greenlee's way. He sat with her for long hours in a stupor of self-recrimination that always started with *fool* and ended up with *jackass*.

Near dawn Greenlee reappeared, took pity and motioned his permission for Jess to stay for his examination. Jess sank onto the chair next to Signey's bed and watched. The doctor stroked and tapped at every joint, checking for reflexive motion, then lifted an eyelid and flashed a penlight at her pupil. The next time, on the other eye, Signey groaned and swatted at the light in her sleep.

"Quite a little fighter, your lady," the doctor said.

"Yeah. Quite a fighter."

"She's got a lump on her head the size of a lemon. It'll be plenty sore, but she'll be fine. Look me up around nine o'clock. I'll check her out of here and you can take her home."

She'll be fine. Distractedly Jess rose, stretched out a hand to the doctor and apologized for overreacting.

Dr. Greenlee shook Jess's hand and shrugged. "It goes with the territory."

When the doctor departed and the door swished shut behind him, Jess scraped his fingers over his unshaven beard. He'd called himself fifty kinds of a fool all night, and his opinion on that score hadn't changed one iota by the time dawn appeared.

Time to face a few home truths.

One. They had known each other less than three months.

Two. He'd laid the old pressure on right from the start. *"Fly with me, play with me, work with me, come with me."* Slow down? Stop? *"Hell, no. You stop it if it's a mistake."* I love you, Jess. *"Not good enough, babe."* My life's all upside down. I need time, just a little time, Jess. *"Fine."*

Three. He'd handed her no ultimatums, set no limits, but last night, when she'd told him about Dave's tests, Jess might as well have said, *"Time's up, Sig, old girl, put up or shut up. Believe in me."*

Signey woke a few minutes after Greenlee left. Holding her hand, Jess told her she'd be okay.

She blinked, focused on his face and reached for her head. "My head . . . it hurts, Jess. What—?"

"Your briefcase caught you on the back of the head."

"Oh, God. The plane . . ."

"Shh, babe. It's okay. I've bent it up worse than that myself."

Confusion competed with the pain. Notwithstanding the crazed images that played for attention in her head, all she could see was the rage on Jess's face when the prop bit into the earth. "You were so . . . angry."

"Yeah." Tension tightened his jaw. It had taken watching her bringing in his bird after the landing gear failure to make him understand at last the kind of heart-stopping, mind-shrieking, gut-searing fear she suffered when he worked a rodeo arena.

There'd been nothing pretty about it. He'd watched, horror stricken and unable to peel his eyes off the plane, and it wasn't the plane he gave a simple damn about.

"Jess. What's wrong?"

The tremor in her well-trained voice was wrong. The swelling on her head was wrong, the starched sheets scraping her skin and the strawberry-blond hair, saturated and stringy with Betadine and alcohol were wrong.

Jess clung to Signey's hand. It felt as cold as winter. There were guts, and then there were guts. He had the kind it took to do what he had to do in a rodeo arena. Now he'd discovered he didn't have the sort it took to face Signey while he explained that it wasn't his bent-up bird that made him so damn mad.

His voice was harsh as only outrage could make it. "I wanted to shake you until your teeth rattled, Signey. The only thing going through my head then was that this was the last one-up stunt you'd ever pull on me. I was the one who was supposed to die first, and you had no business changing the rules."

"Jess, don't . . ."

He remembered the precise moment when he'd known she wouldn't be able to power out of the crash. A part of him wanted to scream that he had never loved her. It would have been easier never to have loved if he'd had to watch her crash and burn and die right there in front of him.

Jess focused on his hands to keep from meeting her eyes. Slowly she pulled her hand from his and stroked at the stubble of whiskers on his jaw. "You need a shave, Hawkins."

"Signey, dammit," he said huskily. "Haven't you heard a word . . . ? Do you understand what I've said?"

A broken sound escaped her throat. "Yes. Forever isn't in the cards." She could barely think; pain still swamped her head, but she understood very well. He was letting her go, because at last he understood her fear.

He wouldn't make one unending ordeal of her life.

12

SIGNEY THREW HERSELF into her new position at the Vegas news bureau. She discovered a flair for publicity and a talent for negotiating deals. There had never been a time in her life when she'd been more busy or the potential for professional satisfaction more heady.

She told herself she was happy, allowed herself not one daylight moment for regrets, and made quite a mental case for things having turned out just as they should.

Life was swell.

But on the day Finley's trial was set to begin, the moment she saw Jess on the courthouse steps in Carson City, she knew life wasn't so swell at all. Climbing out of the taxi she'd taken from the airport, Signey smiled and waved, hugged Dave and envied Kelly the contentment in her eyes and shook hands with Dave's lawyer. Then she turned around and there was Jess. He folded her hands between his, kissed her cheek, and Signey finally faced facts. The late-autumn morning was cold. The sun shone brilliantly. The Nevada skies were a robin's-egg blue and cloudless.

And Signey Jensen would never be free of Jess Hawkins.

She returned his friendly kiss, squeezed his friendly fingers, perhaps a little too tightly, and set about figuring out, perhaps a little too desperately, how to be best friends with the only man she would ever love.

She sat beside him in the first row behind the prosecutor's table while they listened to the testimony documenting the shaky state of Finley's financial empire, the latest developmental technology, and all the possible ways to sabotage a race car.

She listened, but she didn't really hear. Jess held her hand, or else his arm rested behind her. It would have been smarter by far to sit at opposing ends of the row.

Still, they were both skilled at playing games, and this one, pretending they could be just friends, was the ultimate blindman's bluff.

Signey's testimony was scheduled toward the end. In fact, the trial had been going on for two days before she arrived.

This was the last day, and Mancouso shot off everything in his arsenal to discredit her, but it wasn't until he'd almost done that she got the worst of his derision.

"Ms. Jensen, do you find nothing that smacks of misplaced loyalty, here? Does the fact that you were employed by Walter Finley for more than a decade mean nothing to you?"

"To my peers at Cable Sports, of course," she answered. "To Walter Finley himself? I find blind loyalty a fault, sir. I always have."

Thereupon he pointed out to the jury her conflict of interest, her unprofessional conduct and penchant for making trouble. The prosecutor objected, but Mancouso just smiled a worthless apology to the court and passed assorted photographs among the jury members, while his sidekick displayed a blowup of a photo of Jess kissing her in the arena for the entire courtroom to see.

"Tell me, Ms. Jensen, did you have fun rolling around in the mud on your last assignment with Cable Sports?"

Her eyes darted to Jess, and she could almost feel his heart thudding painfully in his chest, because hers thudded as strongly. Suddenly she knew that for Jess, everything about them, everything they had been together, everything they were together was reduced to this moment. *"Tell me, Ms. Jensen, did you have fun?"*

Remembering, Signey shivered. Joy. It all came back to Hawkins's capacity for joy, for creating joy in her. So elemental, so rare a quality.

"Your Honor," Mancouso barked, "would you direct the witness to answer the question!"

The prosecutor roared another objection, but Mancouso argued a serious lack of professional judgment in the prosecution's witness and begged an answer.

Wearily banging his gavel, the judge overruled the objection. "Ms. Jensen?"

Signey's palms grew damp, and she clutched the hem of her emerald-green skirt. She could lie for the sake of maintaining her credibility, or she could tell the truth.

For the sake of joy and old times.

"Yes, Mr. Mancouso. I had a great deal of fun."

Jess's slow, beautiful smile was all that she had lived for, once. Of course, they were just friends now.

But Mancouso wasn't done yet. "One last thing, Signey." It didn't escape anyone's notice that his use of her first name reeked of disrespect. "Will you kindly tell the members of the jury how many offers you've had from other networks for a position similar to the one you held with Cable Sports?"

"None." Signey deliberately released her grip on the hem of her skirt and smoothed out the wrinkles. "I've taken another—"

"*How* many, Signey?" Mancouso feigned enormous surprise and ignored the last of her answer.

"None."

"Doesn't that concern you? Doesn't that tell you something?"

"It tells me, sir," she taunted softly, "that there isn't quite the premium on integrity out there I had supposed."

Mancouso tried to bury the point but Jess grinned broadly, licked one finger and stroked five quick points in the air. The judge banged on his gavel, but it came too late. The jury members, down to the last dour old lady, laughed out loud, and Dave's attorney rose to offer the court the single most unapologetic regrets the judge could ever have heard for the actions of his client's family.

Signey was dismissed from the stand and took her seat next to Hawkins. Each side delivered closing arguments; the jury went into deliberations.

Ninety minutes later the jury returned with a verdict of guilty on seventeen counts of criminal wrongdoing that ran the gamut from fraud to conspiracy to attempted manslaughter. Walter D. Finley et al. were going to jail.

The evening headline touted INTEGRITY in three-inch caps, and everywhere gamblers were paid off against the eight-to-three odds Jimmy Carver had offered. Reno might never again see the likes of the victory party Dave threw at Harrah's.

But Jess took Signey home, and she went because she needed more than anything on earth to prove to herself that she could be friends with him. Just friends.

They hugged and kissed and shouted like old friends over the triumph. All to prove they could touch without the earth shaking.

It trembled but good.

They drove to a small grocery, picked out a piece of meat to make chicken-fried steak, then bought a few potatoes and a boxed lemon-meringue pie. The silence on the way home was friendly. Companionable, Signey decided.

Jess dropped her at the back door, then drove off to feed the livestock. She went inside, changed into jeans she must have left behind in the laundry hamper and a T-shirt of Jess's, and sat down at the kitchen table to peel potatoes with a paring knife, proving how steady were her hands.

If she didn't cut herself, it was because the hand holding the potato trembled in tandem with the hand wielding the knife.

And when Jess came in through the kitchen door and saw her sitting in his kitchen, saw the small dark circles of her nipples plainly through the fabric of his T-shirt, and saw the way her tongue darted out to moisten her suddenly bone-dry lips—well, any man's cords would have seemed suddenly two sizes too small.

He shed his sheepskin coat and gloves and tossed the Blazer keys onto the counter, then sat down and held up his boot for Signey to pull off.

"I've missed you like hell, Signey."

She swallowed hard, dumped the potato and knife into the pot and thumped at the toe of his boot. "You're spoiled, Hawkins."

He grinned, because if he hadn't he'd have slammed his mouth onto hers and to hell with being friends. When she had pulled off both boots and sat down across from him, he crossed his feet on the chair between her legs.

"I hear you're doing real well." His feet settled between her breasts. A pulse flickered in the hollow below her throat.

She thought her insides might melt. "Yeah. I am." Such lies. "Did I tell you I've lined up an exhibition of Spanish bullfighters for the national rodeo finals in December?" She glanced up from her careful scrutiny of potato eyes and her chin rose jauntily. "That's *Spanish* bullfighters, Hawkins. The real thing."

Stroking idly, his toes brushed her breasts. Her nipples tightened, rising instantly against the worn fabric of his T-shirt. His eyes fixed on the small swellings. He smiled.

Oh, God, that smile.

"I am the real thing, babe."

A woman who was a friend didn't react like this. A woman with a friend didn't let her eyes stray to a straining pant-fly. A woman ought to get out, or else admit the game was up.

"I can't do this, Hawkins."

"You can do anything, babe."

Why did he refuse to understand? She'd come here knowing, *knowing* they'd end up in each other's arms, making love. She could no more be just friends with Hawkins than she could lie in that courtroom about having fun with him in the mud.

"Nothing has changed, Jess. I haven't changed." He deserved to know that.

He didn't give a hoot in hell. "Tell me about the Spaniards."

She swallowed her protests. Hawkins was a grown man. And smart. He had to know she hadn't changed her mind about sticking around forever. "We've promised the bullfighters a big bash. They want their American counterparts there."

He leaned forward to pull out the tails of the blue shirt he wore from his jeans, then opened the buttons one at a time until the shirt hung loosely at his sides, framing his muscled, still-tanned chest.

"Will you come?"

She meant, would he come to the party, and Jess knew it. He misunderstood on purpose, giving her question a double meaning she hadn't intended. "Count on it, babe."

His breathing grew shallow, while his eyes strayed from the shadows and the thrusting buds of her breasts to her neck, to her dampened lips, to her rounded, achingly feminine shoulders. Pulling back first one foot and then the other, stripping socks off, he worked his bare feet beneath the T-shirt clinging to her breasts, and watched her eyes go all soft and sexy.

"The party, Jess. I meant to the party."

In turn, she brought her leg to rest upon his, hooked her knees over his, and stroked at his tightened, heavy male flesh with her foot. He leaned back, locking his hands behind his head, granting her gently prodding foot greater access. "I've missed you, Signey. Did you think you could come here and that this wouldn't happen?"

"Oh, God." A sigh that might have been his name whispered from her throat. "Is it going to happen in the kitchen?"

"You're cooking."

"I'm serious."

He smiled. "I know."

"You'll be there?" In Vegas, she meant. The party for the Spanish bullfighters.

"I'm already there."

He took her to bed, chicken-fried steak and raw potatoes and boxed lemon pie forgotten.

But by daylight she had called a cab. By the time Jess woke, she'd forced herself onto a flight out of town.

"You see, Jess, I can't forget exactly how good you are...."

SIGNEY WAS IN NEW YORK, negotiating the final details of cable coverage for the national finals of rodeo, on the morning she first threw up her breakfast. She wrote it off as a mild case of the flu.

She was in Louisiana, bidding on a boxing match for one of the major hotel complexes, the night she couldn't sleep for the achiness in her breasts.

She was in Atlanta packing up her condo when she finally admitted to herself that her birth-control pills had failed. She was pregnant. She was carrying Jess's baby.

Being pregnant with Jess's baby was special and terrifying, and changed everything.

If she hadn't known exactly how much he wanted babies, it might have been a different story.

She had several pretty good reasons to cry now, hormones being only the most obvious one.

She puttered and watered plants and arranged her books in different boxes fifteen times and never once cried. That was no surprise, though she'd carefully lost her cloisonné mirror.

She thought about fate and destiny, love and loss and babies, and a man too reckless to love. Then she happened onto Hemingway's volume about the bullfighters, and read until she was bleary-eyed in search of an answer to her unspoken question.

When she found it, she cried till dawn.

THE NATIONAL FINALS of rodeo brought not only the qualified contestants but thousands upon thousands of fans and the press contingent, and there seemed too much to accomplish and so little time to get it done. Especially when thoughts of Jess's baby nestled in her womb had her on the edge of still more tears at any given moment.

There were moments when the telephones at the bureau had fallen silent for the night and hers rang, anyway, but the voice on the other end wasn't baritone, wasn't husky, wasn't Jess's. Moments when she'd make a wisecrack to relieve the tension, expecting a quick, suggestive comeback, only there was none. Moments when someone's eyes would catch her attention because they held a hint of green, but it wasn't the slate green of his passion or the sea green of his humor, nor was it the jade green of his quick, intense interest. All she could think of was what sort of green they'd turn if he knew about the baby.

Hours of her busy days were consumed by rodeo at the arena. There she couldn't keep herself from watching for Jess. It was useless, of course, because when he was there she couldn't fail to pick him out, and when he wasn't, no amount of imagining his lean, powerful, grace-filled movements could imbue another man's body with them. He'd taken on a new clown persona, the Perennial 'Fraidy Cat, scared of everything but the stick horse he wheeled about on, of the Chihuahua "bull" the spider monkey rode, of his own shadow.

His endearing little persona, his mimes, his clowning brought tears of laughter to thousands of fans; they broke her heart. Fear in a clown character could be endearing; for herself it wasn't endearing at all. The fears of the Perennial 'Fraidy Cat became a parody of her own.

He ran, he ducked, he weaved and bobbed and climbed the walls, even scraped holes in the loose arena dirt to bury his head. But through it all, time and again, the harlequin he portrayed fooled himself and saved the cowboy.

She told herself it was just a clown persona, just a character he'd invented for the amusement of the fans. Jess had seen her, she knew that. Awareness linked them, always. Did he think her presence there a bone she threw him? A scrap of belated faith? He trained no smile upon her, spared her no broadly suggestive winks, and she had no business thinking that the Perennial 'Fraidy Cat was a calculated move on Jess's part.

She had no business, either, forgetting the horror of seeing him caught on the horns of that bull in Cheyenne, but when she tried to dredge it up—to make the infant growing in her body believe all the reasons Mommy couldn't marry Daddy, and Baby makes three, happily ever after—the image simply blurred, and all that was left was the good things. She'd no business thinking that way at all.

KIRSTEN MARIE LINDSTROM was born on the third morning of the rodeo finals at 1:47 a.m., and Kelly was home with the baby by next afternoon for dinnertime, eager to show off the baby. The fact that Jess had been invited to dinner as well changed Signey's mind about going. He had to know. He had to love her enough to let her give faking it one more shot.

The little natives were restless, threatening a small-scale civil war when Signey walked in. Cammie and Danny had already been through this kind of rupture from their mom when Jason was born—they'd also had each other. Now, it seemed, Gramma Vic's dictate that they entertain their little brother met with a stone wall of resistance.

"Here." Victoria thrust the whining, insistent little boy into Signey's arms. "I'm busy with dinner."

Signey took one quick peek at Kirsten, then sat down in another wooden rocker across the living room from Kelly, soothing Jason until he fell asleep against her. Her breasts ached like crazy. Leaning her head back, smiling for Kelly's benefit, Signey closed her eyes and listened for the sound of Jess's Blazer.

He must've been preoccupied, deaf, ignorant or blind, he thought. He'd missed seeing the news bureau station wagon Signey drove, and fallen right into the setup.

And then he must've been mesmerized, deaf, ignorant or heart blind for standing there in the living room archway, rooted to the hardwood floor, watching Signey rocking his nephew, breaking down his resolve to stay away from her all over again.

Wrong. All wrong. Damn it to hell, how much more could a man take?

Signey became aware of a change, of tension, of Jess. Opening her eyes, she felt herself flame crimson at the naked need and the open denial in Jess. It was the denial that wrecked her.

Kelly ignored the killer non-verbals. "Jess, hi. Come see your new niece."

He clenched his teeth against telling Kelly exactly what he thought of her transparent interference, strode across the room and touched baby Kirsten's coal-black hair. All the Lindstrom babies had come like that, and grown into towheads. He wondered if his . . . then viciously beat back the wondering. "I'm not going to stay, Kel."

"Yes," she said. "You are."

"Stay the hell out of it, Kelly."

"I can't."

"Yes." He ground out the word. "You can."

Signey burned with humiliation. Surely the awful pounding of her heart would wake little Jason? But without looking toward her again at all, Jess turned and headed out, passing Victoria, who'd come out of the kitchen to greet him. Kelly eased herself out of her rocker and went after him.

Victoria crossed her arms, apparently reading the situation correctly. "Kelly, for Heaven's sake, sit down."

"Mother, just take Kirsten and get out of my way."

"I will not allow—"

But the baby landed in her grandmother's unwilling arms. Signey rose with the deadweight of Jason in her arms and added her protests to Victoria's.

"Kelly, don't—"

"I did this, Signey, and I'm going to undo it or—"

"He's right, Kel. Please don't get involved. It's over. Please. It's . . . over."

"If you two could see yourselves, you'd know there's nothing over about it," Kelly snapped. "See if Jas will stay asleep if you put him to bed, Signey. Please. Humor me."

Dressed in only her bathrobe, Kelly turned on her heel, opened the screen door, stepped onto the porch and called after Jess's retreating figure. "Jess, I only had the baby a few hours ago. Please don't make me come after you any more."

Jess turned midway down the drive. The early-evening sun blazed into his eyes. "Dammit, Kel, get back in the house and get some rest. Where the hell is Dave, anyway?"

"He's sleeping," she yelled, loudly enough to let him know it was going to be one of *those* hassles if that was what it took. "The point is if I needed him he'd be here, which is more than I can say for you right now, bud."

Jess started to defend himself, then gave it up. He hadn't gone a round with Kelly in ten years he hadn't lost, and it didn't look good now, either. He shoved a Texas Aggie cap onto his head and walked back toward Kelly, so the argument wouldn't be heard all over Clark County.

"He oughta be out here, Kel."

Her robe trailing around bare toes, Kelly spoke more quietly now. "He's tired, Jess. He's human. I'm human. You're human. Heroes are human," she chided.

Jess stewed. Kelly knew damn good and well that line was exactly what had sent him looking for Signey in the first place. Didn't she know, couldn't she see how torn up he was, how badly it went down? "You don't fight fair, Kel."

"I don't want to fight with you at all, Jess. I want to know why you can't come back in and make it up with Signey."

Everything in him wanted to do what Kelly asked, to go back in there and *by damn* fix things up with Signey. He could, and it would all be so simple. Three words, *I'll quit bullfighting*, would do it. It was the quick-fix, stopgap thing to do. Need urged him toward the easy solution. Even the clown in him, the 'Fraidy Cat, lobbied, *"Just fix it."*

He couldn't ignore the overpowering feeling that asking Signey to fake living up to his expectatons anymore was like expecting baby Kirsten to walk tomorrow. *He* knew Signey could, he'd seen and loved the fighter in her himself. But *she* didn't know it, even now. And even now that realization felt like a hot branding iron searing into his chest.

His voice grew hoarse with his frustration. "Kel, if it had been Signey coming out here after me, it might have stood a chance. Don't you see? She has to be the one."

"No. I don't see it, Jess. But you've backed yourself up against the wall and you're going to regret it, if you don't think of something."

"I already regret it, Kel. I already do."

"Don't rest on your laurels, Jess," Kelly warned. She thumped at the bill on his cap, then drew her robe a little tighter around herself and talked to him in the language he knew best. Games. "You're eyeball-to-eyeball with something bigger than just yourself, Jess. Don't blink now."

HE WANTED to get rip-roaring drunk. Wanted to tie one on that'd last till spring, spare him the decision, the pain of cutting loose from Signey. Or not. But as he sat in a little, out-of-the-way cantina, tossing down a single-shot tequila, he admitted to himself, at least, that he wanted something else far more. He wanted not to blink, and the only way he knew how was to go for it instead.

His options in this game of poker he'd begun with Signey had run out. He couldn't hold, couldn't fold, and couldn't run. He could sure as hell call for the showdown.

There might still be one way to win, one way to force her hand. He switched to a soda and lime twist because the plan taking shape in his mind scared him witless. Suddenly, the scheme reshaped itself into a something even he couldn't believe. It surprised him to know he could even think about losing the battle to win the war. Or losing the battle and the war. Before Signey, the only skirmishes he'd even dreamed of losing were the ones with Kel.

Now, when all was said and done, he'd either have his forever, or Signey would tell him to go straight to hell. But he had to do it, as much for her as for himself. He had to get Signey past the fear in her head, past thinking to the point where her heart could make the right decision. In bullfighting circles it was called "Bait and switch."

THE LAST SESSION of the national finals rodeo opened to a roaring, standing-room-only crowd of 16,500. Signey directed traffic, the photographers and reporters gearing up to get a feel for the crowd; a sense of excitement was building as rodeo cowboys brought out their best for the finals. Vendors hawked their programs. Little kids strutted their stuff in jeans and spangled Western wear. Hopes rode sky-high.

Round after grueling round, one man emerged the victor. For every cowboy who won, a dozen only came close. The announcer hyped the crowd time and again. "Close only counts in horseshoes and hand grenades, my friends. Let's give these men the appreciation they deserve."

Signey watched Jess console losers and congratulate winners all afternoon.

Jess watched Signey and hoped against hope he'd get a chance to put his plan into action. He had more at stake than any contestant here. The 'Fraidy Cat was gone, and he'd become Fearless in Flight. Tension gnawed at his guts.

A round of bull riding began at four o'clock. Ten men would have a go at the eliminator pen. "Tough, nasty, uncanny critters, there hasn't been but a handful of men ever ride these animals to the whistle," said the announcer. Like the rest of the crowd, Signey was on her feet.

Kneeling before the chute gates, primed for action, Jess caught the eye of his barrel man and nodded. Anytime now. Whichever bull presented him with the first chance.

His concentration trebled. The first bull blew out of the chute with incredible power. Jess clenched and released his fingers. The crowd began holding its collective breath. Jess blew his out and drew another. The bull twisted and bucked off the ground in a single, awe-inspiring leap. The cowboy went down a full three seconds short of the whistle. Jess moved in.

He sprang forward to meet the bull's rage, taunting the beast toward himself and away from the rider.

The crowd went wild but the bull gave up, snorted and threw up its head, refusing to come at Jess. The hazers moved in to shoo the animal out of the arena. Jess ran his fingers between his neck and bandanna and let the surge of adrenaline seep away.

The next three contestants rode to the whistle. No ride scored all that well, and no bull gave Jess or his cohort much of a fight. The crowd responded with ever-increasing tension. Signey felt every nerve in her body respond with an eerie sense of immediacy, of foreboding.

Jess grew impatient. Not until the last bull was run into the pen did he feel right, but when the bull called

Cyclops exploded out of the chute gate, he knew this was it. His body tensed, his breathing grew deeper.

The bull drilled its rider into the dirt in four seconds. Jess felt time expand as the animal sought a target for its temper. He went with the feeling, recognized the moment to zero in with his concentration. He didn't have to lure, taunt or manipulate this critter. Jess ran fifty feet away, turned and waited. Seconds crawled by. The bull lowered its head, pawed at the earth and charged. Jess held his ground, became rooted, stared into the bull's eyes as it charged, and focused every instinct on holding the position.... Brinksmanship.

The crowd went wild. It might have been a stunt, but it looked like real trouble. He dropped at the last possible second, and in that precise instant his partner cut through to head the animal off in still another direction.

Time hung suspended between one heartbeat and the next for Signey. A hush settled over the crowd when Jess stood up, wooden and still as death.

When the bull was safely shooed out of the arena, Jess wrapped his fists into balls of barely restrained energy, let the adrenaline rush drain out of him and remained standing stock-still. A hush settled over the crowd, then Jess threw his hat into the dirt and walked out of the arena. Sixteen thousand people were convinced this had been no stunt. Hawkins was a beaten man.

Once before she'd experienced the silence, the utter unspeakable silence in her head. The day Jess had been mangled beneath the hooves, on the horns of the bull in Cheyenne. Now the same silence descended upon her. But this was the silence of . . . of peace.

A peace like nothing she had ever known. Maybe it was the baby Hawkins knew nothing of, maybe the fact that she couldn't even now imagine Hawkins hurt. Whatever; she recognized a Hawkins one-up stunt when she saw it. He'd done it for her. The rest was all show, too.

Her heart pounded, and she could have sworn she felt the thumb-sized baby growing in her clapping its tiny little hands with joy. Mommy would just marry Daddy, after all, and Baby'd make three. But Hawkins would pay. If she'd learned nothing else, she'd learned the value of coming back at him with a one-up gambit to top his.

She took her sweet time about getting out of the bureau box seats, down the ramp and under the stands. She found him stripping out of his suspenders, viciously attacking the elastic.

She leaned against the opposite wall with a nonchalance that came out of the incredible peace inside her. "That was one brilliant maneuver, Jess. I've never seen it before, have I?"

He glared at her as if she'd suddenly lost all her wits. "I don't know what you're talking about, Signey."

"Of course you do," she scolded, smiling.

Hell, she's smirking, Jess thought. But the smile faded from her eyes, and the only thing left to him was something to believe in, if he could believe.

"You were faking it. But don't get me wrong, Hawkins. I know what you were doing out there and I know why." There was a sort of hunger in his eyes, a daring to think forever was in the cards, that for the first time she treasured more than she feared. "I'm really quite clever, you know, and people say I'm intuitive. I—"

"Signey." Jess let the suspenders slip from his hands. "Cut to the chase, babe."

Her eyes bored straight into his. "This was a stunt, wasn't it, Jess? Pure showmanship to prove to me once and for all that I could handle things. You did it so I would come down here and make you see you have to go back out into that arena. The Perennial 'Fraidy Cat was great, Jess, but I fell in love with Fearless in Flight."

His heart was knocking around worse than when he'd stood there, letting that bull come straight at him. Back to measuring time in heartbeats. It was her "Gotcha" smile that cut him off at the pass. He began to suspect he'd been had, to feel the joy swelling in him. "And?"

"And I'll go you one better, Hawkins. The party for the Spanish bullfighters is tonight. Seven o'clock. Be there."

JESS SHOWED UP at her condo at something before seven. Signey came to the door, wearing the dress he'd bought her in Cheyenne.

Jess stepped inside, then stood back and hooked his thumbs into his belt. Casual-like, like nothing he felt. "Maybe you should get a wrap. The night air is a little cold."

Was it his imagination, or did her breasts fill the bodice of her dress . . . differently? He hadn't touched her in weeks; he'd have to touch her to know.

Complying, Signey got a shawl out of her coat closet and handed it to him. She hadn't missed the movement of his eyes to her breasts. He'd noticed even this infinitesimal change. He simply didn't know why.

He would know soon. Soon he would know for himself by the measure of his hand. Joy washed through her like sunshine through shadow.

She had never looked more beautiful, never touched his heart more thoroughly, never had the hint of such a sweet promise about her. He watched her as he drove, wondering if he needed a reality check in the worst way. He watched while she sparkled for his friends, as if there were no tomorrow. And he watched her watching him as she turned down dancing offers left and right. He had to wait for her to go him one better, and the suspense was killing him.

The visiting bullfighters took to the microphone and story telling like the scene-stealers they were. The one whose father had known Hemingway teased Signey mercilessly, because it was so ridiculously obvious she was in love with the American bullfighter.

"Don't start being friends with bullfighters again, and especially not with this one, when you know how good he is and how much you will have to lose if anything happens to him."

As if she'd planned this moment to the smallest detail, Signey smiled. The only unplanned bit was the trembling of her lip. "Pay attention, Hawkins. This is where you get yours."

She'd probably counted on his heart thundering along like a herd of mustangs, which was why she gave him the warning. She took to the stage, appropriated the microphone and spouted Hemingway right back at the astonished Spaniard. More, at Jess.

"Fortunately I have never learned to take the good advice I give myself, nor the counsel of my fears."

And then the tears. He could think of five times he'd wished she could just cry. Her tears erased the last vestiges of doubt. Signey Marie Jensen was crying real tears.

Then she handed the microphone back and stood alone, sweet as you please, and if he'd thought his heart had no more room for joy, he learned otherwise. "Take me home, Jess. Pregnant ladies oughtn't be up to all hours."

"Pregnant ladies?" he croaked.

Her eyes opened wide. Innocently. "Yeah, toreador," she sassed. "Pregnant, as in bundle - in - the - oven, barefoot - and - make - an - honest - woman - of - me pregnant."

He fetched her off the stage, held her and felt the swell of her breasts against him, and kissed her there in front of God, his friends and hers.

He'd never been one-upped better, or been so heart-rendingly grateful for God's small favors, either. A baby. His baby.

Their baby. Signey couldn't help her "Gotcha" smile.

"Ah, *señor toreador,*" Jess's Spanish counterpart crooned. "I ask you. Does life get any sweeter than this?"

"No, my friend," Jess replied. "This is as sweet as it gets."

HARLEQUIN Temptation

LOVE AND LAUGHTER

Look for:

Delightful, entertaining, steamy romps. All you expect from Harlequin Temptation—and humor, too!

SLIP BETWEEN THE COVERS...

NEW-1

HARLEQUIN *Temptation*

Rebels & Rogues

All men are not created equal. Some are rough around the edges. Tough-minded but tenderhearted. Incredibly sexy. The tempting fulfillment of every woman's fantasy.

When it's time to fight for what they believe in, to win that special woman, our Rebels and Rogues are heroes at heart.

Josh: He swore never to play the hero . . . unless the price was right.

THE PRIVATE EYE by Jayne Ann Krentz. Temptation #377, January 1992.

Matt: A hard man to forget . . . and an even harder man not to love.

THE HOOD by Carin Rafferty. Temptation #381, February 1992.

At Temptation, 1992 is the Year of Rebels and Rogues. Look for twelve exciting stories about bold and courageous men, one each month. Don't miss upcoming books from your favorite authors, including Candace Schuler, JoAnn Ross and Janice Kaiser.

Available wherever Harlequin books are sold. RR-1

HISTORICAL

STORIES·1991

Bring back heartwarming memories of Christmas past,
with Historical Christmas Stories 1991, a collection of
romantic stories by three popular authors:

Christmas Yet To Come
by Lynda Trent

A Season of Joy
by Caryn Cameron

Fortune's Gift
by DeLoras Scott

A perfect Christmas gift!

HARLEQUIN
American Romance®

From the Alaskan wilderness to sultry New Orleans . . . from New England seashores to the rugged Rockies . . . American Romance brings you the best of America. And with each trip, you'll find the best in romance.

Each month, American Romance brings you the magic of falling in love with that special American man. Whether an untamed cowboy or a polished executive, he has that sensuality, that special spark sure to capture your heart.

For stories of today, with women just like you and the men they dream about, read American Romance. Four new titles each month.

HARLEQUIN AMERICAN ROMANCE—the love stories you can believe in.

my VALENTINE 1992

Celebrate the most romantic day of the year with
MY VALENTINE 1992—a sexy new collection of four
romantic stories written by our famous Temptation
authors:

GINA WILKINS
KRISTINE ROLOFSON
JOANN ROSS
VICKI LEWIS THOMPSON

My Valentine 1992—an exquisite escape into a romantic
and sensuous world.

 Harlequin Books

VAL-92-R

HARLEQUIN
PROUDLY PRESENTS
A DAZZLING NEW CONCEPT IN ROMANCE FICTION

One small town—twelve terrific love stories

Welcome to Tyler, Wisconsin—a town full of people
you'll enjoy getting to know, memorable friends and
unforgettable lovers, and a long-buried secret that
lurks beneath its serene surface....

JOIN US FOR A YEAR IN THE LIFE OF TYLER

Each book set in Tyler is a self-contained love story;
together, the twelve novels stitch the fabric of a
community.

LOSE YOUR HEART TO TYLER!

The excitement begins in March 1992, with
WHIRLWIND, by Nancy Martin. When lively, brash
Liza Baron arrives home unexpectedly, she moves
into the old family lodge, where the silent and
mysterious Cliff Forrester has been living in seclusion
for years....

WATCH FOR ALL TWELVE BOOKS
OF THE TYLER SERIES
Available wherever Harlequin books are sold